I

Fog clung to the Tower, a cloaking mist that shrouded the fortress in a grey-white gloom, its battlements and turrets ghostly silhouettes against the sky. Beyond the bulwarks and ramparts, the Thames lapped at the wharf that lay beneath the ancient keep. The distant creaking of ships at St Katharine Docks and the clatter of their cargo were the only sounds that could be heard as dusk gave way to darkness. Even the guttural croaks of the ravens guarding the Tower had by now fallen silent.

Beneath the arched gateway of the Byward Tower the glow of a lantern could just be glimpsed through the gloom. With a rattle of keys its bearer stepped forward, the sound of his footsteps almost swallowed by the swirling mists as he strode down the narrow cobbled street enclosed between the mighty inner and outer walls of the Tower of London.

The man was dressed in a scarlet uniform, its

flowing sleeves laced around the edges and seams with several rows of gold lace, whilst across his chest the emblem of a crown was set above a rose, shamrock and thistle. His uniform was completed by a low black hat, its broad velvet brim trimmed in a Tudor style.

Behind his prodigious beard, the man's face was set in a solemn expression, his eyes fixed dead ahead as he carried out the duties of the Chief Warder. The blank stares of the narrow windows set high on the Bell Tower watched him as he passed, bearing witness to a ceremony that had been performed every night for the past six hundred years: the locking up of the Tower of London.

As the warder approached the archway beneath the Bloody Tower, its name a grisly testament to the fate of the traitors brought through its gates, he could see the shadowy forms of four figures standing sentry in the darkness. These guards were dressed in dark-blue uniforms, rifles shouldered as they stood to attention. The towering shadows cast by their black bearskin hats gave them the look of strange giants in the gloom.

Without breaking his stride, the Chief Warder handed his lantern to the guardsman at the rear of this small escort then took up his position between the two leading guards. The bark of their sergeant cut through the creeping fog.

"Escort to the Keys! By the centre – quick march!"

Marching in step with his escort, the warder led the way across the cobbled stones back to the outer gate. Swinging the towering gates shut with a slam, the guardsmen hefted the huge hasps into place, sliding the bolts across as, with a rattle of his keys, the warder locked and secured the gates for the night. The escort marched on, repeating this ceremony as they locked the great oak gates of the Middle and Byward Towers. Since the first foundation stone had been laid, the Tower of London had been a fortress, a palace and a prison: the home of princes and kings and the place of their torture. The days when the King took residence here were long gone, but the garrison of soldiers at the base of the Tower remained to guard the Crown Jewels that were still kept here, locked behind stone walls twelve feet thick in the Wakefield Tower.

As the escort stepped again through the archway beneath the Bloody Tower, a cry rang out from the shadows.

"Halt! Who comes there?"

A lone sentry stood by the guardhouse at the base of the Wakefield Tower, his rifle thrust forward as pale wisps of mist curled round the exposed steel of its bayonet. The warder's heels clicked to a halt as he called out his reply.

"The Keys."

"Whose keys?" came the question.

With a solemn authority, the Chief Warder's voice cut through the thickening fog.

"King Edward's keys."

Shouldering his rifle, the sentry snapped to attention.

"Advance, King Edward's keys, and all's well."

The warder stepped forward a single pace, then raised his hat high in the air.

"God preserve King Edward the Seventh."

As a clock chimed eleven, the escort raised their rifles in salute, a chorus of "Amen" echoing off the stones. But the sound of this quickly turned to a cry of consternation as a shadowy figure stumbled down the steps leading from the Wakefield Tower. Dressed in a long dark coat, the figure lurched forward as if weighed down by an unnatural burden. At the guardhouse at the base of the tower, the sentry swivelled to face this unexpected intruder.

"Halt! Who comes there?" he called out, a slight tremor of uncertainty in his voice.

The shadowy figure gave no answer as he stumbled across the cobblestones, his heavy coat bulging as if concealing something hidden within. Behind him, unnoticed by the guards, the dark shapes of other figures, similarly encumbered, flitted through the gloom, slipping between the shadows before disappearing into the darkness. As the first figure lurched towards the Byward

Tower, the Chief Warder stepped forward to challenge him, the ring of keys still jangling in his grasp. It was his duty to secure the Tower and he would make sure that this mysterious interloper passed no further. His accompanying escort raised their rifles in concert, taking aim as the warder stepped into the intruder's path.

"Halt! I command you to identify yourself."

His path barred, the shambling figure raised his head to meet the Chief Warder's stern gaze. Beneath a low black cap, his features were hidden behind a muffling scarf, the black material wrapped around his face. In the jaundiced glow of the lantern's light, the intruder's eyes could just be glimpsed, darting nervously towards the locked gates of the Byward Tower, a dozen steps or so beyond the warder's portly frame.

"I said, identify yourself," the warder snapped. He reached out a crimson-clad arm to snatch at the scarf hiding the intruder's features. As the material unravelled in his hand, the Chief Warder's rasp of challenge quickly turned to a low gasp of fear. Beneath the disguise, the nervous face of a young man stared out, his unlined features barely out of boyhood. But this wasn't the reason the warder stepped back in alarm. Beneath the low brim of his cap, the boy's features shone with a peculiar green glow, a strange luminescence illuminating his skin as if it was lit from within. In the flickering shadows of the Tower, it looked more like some spectral countenance than the face of a mortal man.

"Heaven preserve us," the warder breathed. "What are you?"

In reply, the young man pushed past him, the touch of his fingers sending a burning sensation racing up the older man's arm. Gasping in pain, the Chief Warder fell to his knees, the embroidered keys on the sleeve of his scarlet uniform scorched beyond recognition.

The guardsmen called out for the intruder to halt, taking aim with their rifles as his shadowy figure stumbled towards the Byward Tower. The broad oak gates there were locked and bolted, their ancient defences so strong that even an invading army could not breach them. The fleeing figure didn't even slow his step as a second shout of warning rang out, the edge of his shadow almost at the gate.

"Fire!"

With a splutter of cracks, a volley of shots cut through the gloom, the smoke from the soldiers' carbines thickening the mist even as the bullets flew. As the sound of the rifle fire faded, a chorus of shouts rang out from the battlements, their echoes heard from every corner of the Tower, raising the fortress from its slumber.

"Sound the alarm! Sound the alarm!"

Their rifles still raised, the guards advanced beneath the archway of the Byward Tower. The huge hasps and bolts of the locked gates were still in place, fresh splinters of oak gouged from the solid timber where the bullets had hit home. As the lantern cast a sallow light across the scene, the guards searched the shadows for any sign of the intruder, expecting to find his body slumped across the cobblestones. But the darkness lay empty, only mocking fingers of mist taunting the guards with their failure. The man had simply disappeared.

As a clamour of alarm bells filled the night air, the sound of an anguished shout turned the gazes of the searching guardsmen back towards the Byward Tower, a sudden look of fear written across each of their faces.

"The Crown Jewels are gone!"

Penelope stared down at the blank sheet of paper in front of her, its expanse of perfect whiteness an unconquered continent of story. She felt like Captain Scott staring out from the prow of the *Discovery* at the looming Antarctic coastline, strange mountains of ice barring the way to his goal. Penny sighed, her gaze slipping sideways to the wastepaper basket beside her desk. Balls of crumpled paper spilled out from it, the unfinished sentences scrawled across each sheet a journal of her failure to capture even a foothold in this new tale she was trying to craft from the pen of Montgomery Flinch.

Penny brushed a stray strand of hair from her eyes. Her long dark hair was piled high upon her head in the very latest style. The exquisite tailoring of her pea-green suit seemed more suited to the salons of high society than this dusty old office, its desks and cabinets piled high with papers. The mocking scratch of a pen drew

Penny's gaze to the rear of the room where her guardian, Mr Wigram, sat hunched over a ledger of accounts. The elderly lawyer's pen scurried across the page as he calculated items of income and expenditure, the frown lining his brow telling Penelope all she needed to know about the state of *The Penny Dreadful*'s finances.

The halcyon days of the turn of the century were gone, and with them the success *The Penny Dreadful* had known when sales had topped a million copies and made Montgomery Flinch a household name. Back then his stories of terror and suspense had gripped the nation, long lines of readers queuing at the bookstands to get their hands on the next instalment of his latest macabre tale. Penelope's mind had been a constant whirl of dark imaginings: *A Night in the Gallery*, *The Strange Fate of Doctor Naylor*, *The Gravedigger's Revenge* – every new tale that she told an even greater success than the last. But then the spark of inspiration had started to wane, her ideas for new stories failing to ignite as soon as she tried to chase them on to the page. Montgomery Flinch's pen had fallen silent at last.

In his absence, *The Penny Dreadful*'s sales had fallen into a sad decline. Penelope had commissioned new writers to fill the void: Oliver Onions, William Hope Hodgson, Edward Benson to name but a few, each author trying to replicate the thrilling mix of mystery and the macabre that Montgomery Flinch had mastered, but the readers had simply moved on. Since the death of Queen Victoria more than a year ago, it seemed as though the public's tastes had changed. Tales of crime and detection were now all the rage, filling the pages of *The Penny Dreadful*'s rivals. Even Sherlock Holmes himself had made a belated comeback in *The Hound of the Baskervilles*.

Penny's gaze flicked up to the bookcase behind her guardian's desk, the collected editions of *The Penny Dreadful* taking pride of place there. If the magazine's sales continued on their downward spiral, the latest annual volume with the dates January–December 1901 picked out in gold letters against its crimson spine might be the very last. *The Penny Dreadful* needed something big to restore its sales to their former glory. It needed a story from Montgomery Flinch.

Penelope's gaze returned to the page, her mind a similar blank. All she needed was an idea, the spark for a story, but inspiration remained cruelly elusive. With a tut of irritation, she crumpled up the blank sheet of paper and tossed it into the wastepaper basket where it joined the rest of her unfinished tales. At the sound of this, Mr Wigram lifted his head.

"A problem with the new story?" he asked, fixing Penelope with a solicitous stare.

A frown furrowed Penny's brow but before she had a chance to reply, the rattle of the door handle announced Alfie's arrival. Swinging the door open, the printer's assistant bowled into the office with a grin, the galley proofs for the latest edition of *The Penny Dreadful* tucked under his arm.

"Hello, Penny; afternoon, Mr Wigram."

Alfie stepped towards Penelope's desk, his slicked-back blond hair gleaming in the sunlight that spilled in from the street outside before the front door slowly swung shut again.

"The June edition of *The Penny Dreadful*," he announced, placing the proofs in front of her.

"You're late," Wigram replied in a reproachful tone. "I sent you out to collect those proofs from the printers over an hour ago."

With a wince, Alfie glanced up to meet the lawyer's gimlet gaze.

"I'm sorry, Mr Wigram," he began, "but it's really not my fault. The streets are being dug up left, right and centre – Pall Mall, the Strand, Piccadilly – I had to double-back on myself half a dozen times before I even reached the printers. It's all for the King's coronation, you see. They want every inch of the carriage route looking spick and span before the 26th of June."

He turned back towards Penelope, his eyes shining with excitement.

"You should see the decorations, Penny! There are garlands hanging from every lamppost – flags and flowers everywhere. They've even built a huge archway across Whitehall, fifty feet or so high, all lit up with electric lights. It's magnificent. Trust good old Teddie to show the world how to throw a party!"

As Alfie enthused about the preparations for King Edward the Seventh's forthcoming coronation, Penny stared down at the pile of proofs. On the inside leaf of the front cover, the announcement that she now dreaded stared back at her in bold black type:

MONTGOMERY FLINCH IS BACK!

The Penny Dreadful is proud to announce the long-awaited return of the Master of the Macabre to its pages with a thrilling new tale. This mystery from the pen of Montgomery Flinch, whose absence from the world of fiction has been keenly felt by his many readers, will be found equal, if not superior, in chilling intent to the very best of those tales which first made his name.

"TITLE HERE" will appear in the July edition of *The Penny Dreadful*.

Penny sighed. The deadline for the July edition was little more than a month away. Five weeks to conjure a story out of nothing. At the sound of her sigh, Alfie glanced down, following her gaze to the announcement on the page.

"Don't worry," he said, pulling out a sharpened pencil from behind his ear. "That last line is just a placeholder. As soon as you let me know the actual title of your new story I can mark up the proofs and send the magazine to press."

Penelope looked up to see Alfie's eager smile, his pencil poised above the proof.

"There is no title," she replied, pushing herself back from her desk with an exasperated sigh. "There is no new story." Her gaze flicked from Alfie to her guardian, puzzled looks slowly spreading across both their faces. "I've racked my brain trying to dream up a fitting plot, but it's no use. Every thought that I've had has been written a thousand times before: tales of unquiet spirits, omens and forewarnings. The world has moved on and Montgomery Flinch's fiction needs to as well, but what shape this new story should take is a mystery to me. My fingers itch to write, but my mind remains a blank." With worry lining her brow, Penny glanced across to meet her guardian's gaze. "What should I do?"

For a moment Mr Wigram remained silent, his lips pursed in contemplation as he steepled his fingers beneath his chin. Then with a sigh that almost sounded like relief, he gave his reply.

"You must abandon this plan to bring Montgomery Flinch back to the pages of *The Penny Dreadful*. There really is no need to put yourself under this pressure, Penelope." His wizened features creased in a look of avuncular concern. "Perhaps it is now time to put your writing to one side and seek out other more suitable pursuits. In less than six months' time you will be sixteen years of age and I cannot help but think that your father would reproach me if he knew how I had allowed you to neglect your education to attend instead to the demands of *The Penny Dreadful*. With the investments I have made on your behalf, you are now a young lady of some considerable means. It will soon be time for you to make your entrance into society. Let us lay Montgomery Flinch to rest at last and leave these tales of the macabre behind."

Penelope scowled at her guardian's suggestion. Her gaze flicked up to Alfie's face, seeking out her friend's support, but she saw instead only a sudden blush colouring his complexion.

"I will not abandon *The Penny Dreadful*," she replied, her gaze returning to meet Wigram's own. "Besides, the announcement of Montgomery Flinch's return has already been placed in the pages of *The Times*, *The Sketch* and *The Illustrated London News*. Montgomery Flinch will write again – all I need is a spark of inspiration to set my imagination ablaze."

"Bravo!" Alfie clapped his hands together delightedly, but then his applause quickly faded as Wigram cast him a glowering stare. "I just mean to say that Penny's right – this is what the world is waiting for. Ever since the announcement was made, people keep pestering me everywhere I go – all asking the same question about Montgomery Flinch's new serial." Alfie met Penny's gaze with a look of devoted pride. "They've not forgotten the frights that you gave them before and are eager to find out more about this new mystery. Some are even dreaming up their own stories in anticipation of what Flinch will write. If I had a penny for every idea that I heard, I could double my wages in a day: phantom coaches, ghostly doubles, clocks that strike thirteen. Old Charley at the print shop says that Flinch should tell the story of the printer's devil who haunts that place in his next tale. He told me that the ghost of an apprentice sometimes appears before the printing presses roll. Apparently this poor devil was crushed to death in the press when Charley was only an apprentice himself, but Charley swears blind that whenever there's a rush job on, his friend's ghost returns to try and help him set the type again. Charley says that any typographical errors we find in the proofs of *The Penny Dreadful* are where the printer's devil has left his mark." Alfie shivered. "I reckon he's just trying to put the wind up me though and shift the blame for any shoddy workmanship."

Penelope sighed. It seemed as if the whole world knew what Montgomery Flinch should write next, but she was left without a clue. Alfie's well-meant words rang with a mocking echo inside her mind. *If I had a penny for every idea that I heard...*

As she stared down at the announcement again, a tiny spark glinted in her eyes. The idea was so simple, it was almost ridiculous. The ghost of a smile crept across her lips. Snatching the pencil from Alfie's fingers, Penny began to score through the lines of the announcement, scribbling her corrections in the margins as Alfie watched on intrigued. With a puzzled frown, Wigram rose from his chair, stepping across the office to join them as his ward looked up from the proofs with a grin.

"What do you think?" she asked.

Alfie craned his head towards the page, quickly deciphering Penelope's annotations with an expert eye.

MONTGOMERY FLINCH IS BACK!

The Penny Dreadful is proud to announce the long-awaited return of the Master of the Macabre with news of a thrilling competition. The once-in-a-lifetime chance to see your idea for a story turned into the plot of Montgomery Flinch's newest tale. Could you dream up a mystery fit for the pages of *The Penny Dreadful*? Send your entries to the offices of *The Penny Dreadful*, 38 Bedford Street, London.

All entries must be received by the 21st of May 1902, and the winning entrant will have the chance to meet Montgomery Flinch and see their suggestion transformed into the lead story of the July edition of *The Penny Dreadful*.

Wigram raised a sceptical eyebrow as Alfie finished reading the announcement aloud.

"A competition." He sniffed. "Are you sure this is wise, Penelope?"

Pursing her lips in a stubborn line, Penny nodded her head in reply.

"If what Alfie says is true, we will be deluged with entries – *The Penny Dreadful*'s readers won't be able to resist the chance to see their ideas turned into a story by the illustrious Montgomery Flinch." Her pale-green eyes shimmered with a renewed sense of purpose. "And I only need the right spark of inspiration to fire my imagination into life once more."

III

Beneath a cloudless sky, an expectant hush fell over the red-brick pavilion, its crisp white balconies affording the spectators seated there the finest view of the field of play. Out in the centre of the velvet-green oval, a batsman stood guard at his wicket, the cricketing whites of the opposing team clustering closer as the bowler marked out his run-up.

As the sun beat down on his candy-striped cap, Arthur Conan Doyle tapped his bat against the crease in anticipation of the delivery to come. With a walrus moustache perched atop his upper lip and his broad shoulders set in a resolute stance, the distinguished figure of Doyle looked like an immovable object positioned in front of his stumps. On the scoreboard, his batting tally was recorded in double figures, only three runs shy of his century.

AUTHORS V. ARTISTS

BATSMAN	RUNS
DOYLE A C	9 7

Beginning his run-up, the bowler hurried across the turf, his galloping stride picking up pace as he thundered to his mark. With a flick of his wrist he bowled his delivery, the ball pitching in the dust before rising towards the wicket in a curling flight. Keeping his eyes fixed on the ball, Doyle swung his bat, connecting with a thwack that sent the delivery high in the sky to the delighted gasps of the crowd of onlookers. The ball soared towards the grandstand, clearing silly mid-off as the fielding team turned to watch its flight.

"It's a six," Alfie exclaimed. "It has to be."

From her seat in the pavilion next to him, Penelope glanced up from the pile of papers perched on her lap. Her hair was pinned up beneath a cap, whilst her boyish attire echoed Alfie's own. This was the price she had to pay for their complimentary seats, all thanks to the Marylebone Cricket Club's ridiculous prohibition on ladies entering the pavilion during play. Penny watched as the ball arced through the sky towards them, the crowd holding its breath, hands poised ready to unleash a thunderous ovation to acclaim the centurion.

But then the ball began to fall, the laws of

physics finally defying Doyle as it dropped, agonisingly short of the boundary rope. The fielder positioned there raised his arm high, brandishing the ball in triumph as his teammates rushed to congratulate him.

With a scowl, Doyle hefted his bat beneath his arm, departing the crease in high dudgeon: the celebrated creator of Sherlock Holmes dismissed just three runs short of his century. As the crowd's applause accompanied Doyle on his long walk back to the pavilion, Alfie glanced across to see the next batsman already descending the steps from the dressing room. A cream-white sweater strained to contain the batter's portly frame, his pads flapping as he clacked his way down the steps.

"It looks like Monty's in next."

Penny looked up to see the man the world knew as Montgomery Flinch nearing the bottom of the steps. Giving his bat a practise swing, Monty almost brained a young boy who was standing waiting by the boundary gate.

"Ouch!"

With a blush colouring his cheeks, Monty quickly tucked his cricket bat underneath his arm.

"Watch out, my boy," he declared. "You don't want to get in the way of one of Montgomery Flinch's thunderous cover drives, do you?"

Turning, the boy glanced up at Monty with a

scowl, his autograph book and pen still clutched in his hand.

"Here," Monty said in a mollifying tone, holding out his hand for the book. "Let me give you my signature for your collection. You'll be able to tell all your pals that you were there when Montgomery Flinch scored his century."

With a swift shake of his head, the boy hung on to his book.

"No thank you, sir," he replied. "I'm after the autograph of the man who created Sherlock Holmes." The boy turned back towards the gate as it was swung open by the figure of the returning batsman. "Excuse me, Mr Doyle – would you please sign my book for me, sir?"

A thunderous expression still lining his brow, Doyle stooped to take the autograph book with a grunt, scrawling his signature across the open page before returning it to the boy's hands.

"Thank you, sir!" the boy exclaimed, staring down in awe at the signature, before hurrying back to his seat in the stands.

Shaking off his embarrassment at the young boy's snub, Monty stepped forward to greet Doyle.

"Bad luck there, Arthur," he exclaimed. "I think Swinstead must have baffled you with his slower ball. But don't worry, I'll make sure that the Authors have a centurion on the scoreboard before the end of the innings."

Doyle scowled at this reminder that his own wicket had fallen three runs short of this mark.

"Slower ball, I'll be blown," he replied gruffly, his prodigious moustache bristling at Monty's impertinent suggestion. Brushing past him, Doyle stomped up the steps back to the dressing room. Then the crowd's fading applause redoubled again as Monty swung the gate open and stepped out on to the field of play. With a few practice swings of his bat, he strode across the pitch, greeting the opposing team with a nod of his head as he took his position at the crease.

"Come on, Monty," Alfie breathed.

Prodding his bat against the turf, Monty took guard in front of his wicket. His rosy cheeks shone in the sunlight, a testament to the early drinks break he had taken in the dressing room to calm his nerves. Monty's appearance at this match between the Authors and Artists cricket clubs had seemed like the perfect opportunity to reintroduce Montgomery Flinch to the world after his long absence from the public stage. However, as Penny watched the actor fumble his grip on the bat, she couldn't help wonder if she had made a terrible mistake. She sighed, her gaze returning to the pile of papers perched on her lap. At the moment Monty's cricketing prowess was the least of her concerns. Without a story to write, Montgomery Flinch's return was going to be over before it even began.

It wasn't that Alfie's prediction hadn't come true. Indeed, if she had a penny for every story idea that had dropped through the letterbox since the competition had been announced, she would be wealthy enough to merit an invitation to the King's coronation. Her carefully planned advertising campaign in the pages of *The Times*, *The Sketch* and *The Illustrated London News* had done the trick. The office was awash with entries: reams of paper scattered across every desk and piled high atop cabinets. From primly inked letters on lavender notepaper to scrawled submissions on tattered scraps of paper, the competition had captured the readers' imaginations. But Penelope's initial sense of triumph had been short-lived as she began to leaf through the entries. Instead of the sparks of inspiration she hoped to discover, she found instead ridiculous plots filled with wandering ghosts, grotesque beasts and barely credible characters: *The Purple Terror*; *The Man Who Meddled with Eternity*; *The Last Days of London*...

Most of the stories had been plucked wholesale from the pages of *The Penny Dreadful*'s rivals, their readers seemingly having little care for the conventions of copyright law. Some hadn't even bothered to try to think up their own plots and instead just clipped out preposterous newspaper stories, stuffing these reports into envelopes addressed to *The Penny Dreadful*.

Penelope frowned as she recalled some of the more outlandish reports: tales of the sightings of strange wraiths and radiant boys haunting the streets of London. How had she ever imagined she would find the plot for Montgomery Flinch's latest story amid this mound of slush?

So when this chance of a trip to Lord's had presented itself, Penelope had jumped at the chance. It had been a blessed relief to escape from the confines of the office, leaving her guardian, Mr Wigram, behind to glare at the stacks of paper edging across his desk. Now as Monty tapped his bat against the crease, Alfie leaned forward in his seat next to Penny, the crowd's expectant hush suddenly broken by his shout of encouragement.

"Come on, Monty – hit the feller for six!"

The blazers seated around them tutted their disapproval at this outbreak of loutish behaviour, more suited to the football terraces than the hallowed home of cricket. Ignoring them, Alfie watched as the lanky bowler set off on a cantering run towards the stumps. The crowd waited, eagerly anticipating the opening strike of Montgomery Flinch's first innings.

As the ball flew through the air towards him, Monty took a stumbling stride down the pitch, hoiking his bat high with a club-handed flourish. Somehow he connected, willow meeting leather and sending the ball soaring skywards towards the pavilion. A ripple of applause accompanied its flight, Monty watching from the crease with a dazed smile on his face.

This smile faded as swiftly as the ball fell, dropping into the grateful hands of the fielder waiting at deep extra cover. The crowd's applause, which had sounded in anticipation of a six, now greeted a wicket instead. At the crease, a crestfallen Monty tucked his bat under his arm and began the long walk back to the pavilion.

"A duck," Alfie muttered, shaking his head in disbelief. "A golden duck. Oh, Monty..."

As he reached into his pocket to extract his scorecard and pencil, Penelope turned her attention back to her papers, thankful at least that Monty had escaped his innings without causing any serious injuries.

"Oh, I forgot to say," Alfie piped up, peeling an envelope from the back of the scorecard where it had become stuck in the confines of his pocket. "This arrived at the office today, although I'm impressed that it even found its way there at all."

Taking the envelope from him, Penny swiftly saw for herself the reason why. Scrawled across the front where the address should be was a single name, written in a trembling hand.

Montgomery Flinch

Penelope's heart sank. This must be yet another competition entry, this time from someone who could barely even write from the look of it. She unfastened her purse and was just about to place the envelope inside when something on the reverse caught her eye.

It was a sketch of a bird – what looked like a black crow – poised as if it were about to take flight. The cruel curve of its beak was captured in a series of confident lines, while the plumage of its black feathers was picked out with exquisite penmanship. In the pages of *The Penny Dreadful*, Penny had commissioned some of the finest illustrators in London, and this sketch of the black crow was easily their equal.

Intrigued, she slid her fingernail beneath the envelope's seal, careful not to tear the illustration as she drew out the letter that lay inside. Unfolding it, Penelope began to read.

Mr Flinch,

You are the only man in London I can trust with this confession. The newspapers stay silent, but I know The Penny Dreadful will not fear to reveal the truth of this conspiracy.

You must believe me when I say I do not wish to do these things that they ask of me, but when that terrible fire races through my veins I am powerless to refuse. I am a living man, but these experiments are turning me into a ghost. No prison can hold me; no fortress can keep me out. I have even walked through the walls of the Tower to steal for them the King's crown. I dread to think what they will ask of me next.

Please, Mr Flinch, I beg you to help bring my nightmare to an end.

At the bottom of the page, in place of a signature, was a sketch of another black crow. Penelope's mind whirled as she tried to make sense of this strange letter with its talk of confession and conspiracy, treason and robbery. It had all the ingredients she needed for Montgomery Flinch's next story. Her gaze fixed on a single sentence: *I have even walked through the walls of the Tower to steal for them the King's crown.*

Behind Penny's eyes a spark ignited, her imagination finally shaking off the paralysis that had plagued her for these past twelve months. Feverishly, she started to shape these ideas into a plot: a tale of a villain meddling with unknown powers and twisting these to meet his nefarious ends.

It was perfect. If the reading public wanted tales of crime and mystery then she would give them a villain to outshine even Professor Moriarty, and a plot that Sherlock Holmes himself would not be able to solve. The theft of the Crown Jewels by the thief who wasn't there...

Penny's fingers itched as her thoughts raced

ahead, sketching out the characters who would populate her tale. She reached for her notebook inside her satchel, but before she could put pen to paper, the heavy clump of cricket shoes interrupted her train of thought. Penny looked up to see Monty pushing his way through the pavilion crowd to join them. On his arrival, the actor slumped down in the empty seat on Penelope's right-hand side, raising an eyebrow at her boyish disguise as he cast his cricket bat to one side.

"Did you see him?" he grumbled, jabbing his finger towards the gangling figure of the bowler, now pacing out his run-up once again. "His front foot was at least half a yard outside the crease when he bowled that delivery. It was as clear a no-ball as you'll ever see, but that blasted umpire didn't say a word. It's simply not cricket."

Penelope couldn't stop a bemused smile from curling the corners of her lips. In truth, she had understood little of Monty's complaint, but the actor's annoyance at the manner of his dismissal was evident as he angrily untied his pads from around his legs.

Alfie leaned across, a puzzled frown on his brow.

"Er, Monty," he began, keeping his voice low as the bemused spectators watched the esteemed Montgomery Flinch remove his protective apparel in the midst of the pavilion. "Shouldn't you be doing that in the dressing room?"

Monty shook his head.

"What? And listen to the condescending commiserations of Arthur Conan Doyle before he brags about his own near century? No fear," he replied with a snort. "I'd rather watch the rest of the innings from here." Monty's gaze flicked up to the windows of the Long Room Bar. Through the colonnaded windows he could see a group of gentlemen dressed in red-and-gold blazers, their faces turned towards the field of play as they sipped from champagne flutes. Monty turned to Alfie. "Dear boy, would you be good enough to fetch me some refreshments? My exertions have given me quite a thirst."

With a sigh, Alfie rose to his feet, setting his scorecard down as he headed for the bar. Monty settled back in his seat with a grin, the prospect of the early arrival of the drinks interval soothing any remaining annoyance about the manner of his dismissal. He turned towards Penny, the open letter still perched atop the pile of papers in her lap.

"And how goes the search for my next story?" he asked with a twinkle in his eye. "I trust that the tale that you choose will put Conan Doyle's new Sherlock in the shade."

Penny looked up from the letter to meet Monty's gaze.

"Oh yes," she replied with a confident smile. "It will be a bestseller."

IV

Mr Wigram looked up from his ledger, the neatly kept rows of numbers and tallies at last giving him a reason to smile. The ghost of a grin hovered around the corners of his mouth.

"It's a sell-out," he declared. "There isn't a copy of the July edition of *The Penny Dreadful* left on any newsstand in London. The provinces are already clamouring for yet more copies faster than Truscott and Son can print them. I don't quite know how you have done it, Penelope, but with this new tale from the pen of Montgomery Flinch you have restored the magazine's fortunes at a stroke."

Standing by her guardian's side, Penny felt a frisson of pride. She had known as soon as she had put her pen to the page that the tale of *The Thief Who Wasn't There* had the makings of a bestseller, but even she hadn't foreseen what a sensation it would create. In the shadow of the King's coronation, her story of an audacious plot to steal the Crown Jewels had captured the imagination of the nation. And with the character of the Black Crow, a criminal mastermind whose very identity was shrouded in mystery, she had created a fictional villain without equal.

With powers verging on the diabolical, the Black Crow had swept a swathe of villainy through the pages of *The Penny Dreadful*. A gentleman criminal, his features always hidden in the depths of his hooded disguise, the Black Crow could accomplish the impossible. Her story described how he had broken into the heart of the Tower of London, stealing past the soldiers guarding the jewels like a spectre in the night and then walking through walls to make good his escape. The reading public were enthralled by his villainous exploits and now waited with bated breath to see what cunning plot Montgomery Flinch would concoct for him next.

Her thoughts turning again to this very question, Penelope glanced across at Alfie. The printer's assistant sat half hidden behind the stacks of letters piled high on his desk. Feeling Penny's eyes upon him, Alfie looked up from the latest envelope he had opened, meeting her enquiring gaze with a weary shake of his head. There was still no sign of any further missives decorated with the sketch of a black crow.

Penny sighed. With the success of the story of *The Thief Who Wasn't There*, she had expected the anonymous author of the letter that had inspired it to write in again to claim his prize. However, it appeared that the fevered imagination that had disguised his competition entry as a confession, even to the extent of ending his letter with a plea for help, was now, for some reason, reluctant to come forward. Penelope's hopes of picking his brain for fresh inspiration were fading quickly. It looked like she would have to think up her own plot for the Black Crow's next adventure.

The sound of a sharp knock at the door brought her thoughts back to the real world. She turned to see the office door swing open as Monty entered, brandishing a willow bat.

"Anyone for cricket?" he declared, stepping inside with a spring in his step. He was dressed from head to toe in his cricketing whites, a striped blazer flung over one shoulder. As Alfie rose from his seat in excitement, Monty tossed him his cricket bat.

"Give that a shine for me, will you, Alfie," he asked with a smile. "I need this bat in tip-top condition if I'm going to turn out for Conan Doyle's new team. He says that the great W. G. Grace is bringing along an eleven to face us. I catch the train for Esher in an hour."

Alfie raised an eyebrow in surprise.

"I thought that Mr Doyle had said Montgomery Flinch's game was more suited to the village pond than the village green after your pair of ducks in the match at Lord's."

Monty bristled as behind him Penelope tried to smother her smile.

"Arthur assures me that he was misquoted," Monty replied, an indignant blush colouring his cheeks as he recalled the match report. "Besides," he continued, turning now to face his employer, "he has made me a rather exciting offer that I believe will be to your liking, Penelope."

Penny's smile faded slightly.

"An offer?" she enquired.

Monty grinned.

"The chance to make literary history," he replied. Draping his striped blazer on the coat stand, the actor eased himself into the chair behind Penelope's desk. "Arthur has proposed to me that we collaborate on a new story pitting his creation against mine – Sherlock Holmes meets the Black Crow in the ultimate tale of mystery." With a flourish, Monty perched his cricket shoes on the corner of Penny's desk, then reached into his top pocket to draw out a cigar. "A capital idea, I thought."

The swish of her long skirt followed Penelope as she strode across the office. As Monty fumbled for his matchbox, Penny plucked the cigar from his fingers, fixing the actor with an exasperated glare.

"But, Monty, how on earth can you collaborate with Arthur Conan Doyle when you haven't written a single word of a story in your life? The only black crow I have ever seen you take an interest in is the one on the label of your whisky bottle. I trust you haven't agreed to this preposterous proposal?"

Monty's smile wavered.

"Ah, well, the thing is..."

"Oh, Monty!" Penny clapped her hand to her forehead. "How am I supposed to write Montgomery Flinch's part of the story when you and Doyle are ensconced in the confines of your gentlemen's club?"

"Details, details," Monty replied, recovering his bluster with an airy wave of his hand. "I may have to share a few drinks with Arthur at the club as we work out the details of the plot, but when it comes to the serious business of writing then I'll return here to the office and let you work your magic on the page."

Penelope frowned, not fooled by Monty's attempts at flattery.

"Just imagine what a story you could tell," he continued, casting a rueful glance at his confiscated cigar. "To have the Black Crow pit his villainous wits against the famous Baker Street detective – the reading public will be eager to see who gets the upper hand."

Penny glanced around the office to check the reactions of the others to this unexpected proposition. Familiar furrows lined her guardian's brow, but Alfie's face was lit up with a beaming smile.

"Sherlock Holmes versus the Black Crow – you simply have to write that story, Penny."

Penelope pursed her lips as she turned back to face Monty. The idea was an intriguing one, she had to admit that. And the chance to write a Sherlock Holmes adventure was almost too delightful to resist.

Sensing that Penelope's interest was piqued, Monty pressed home the proposal.

"Arthur suggests that we split the publication of the serial between the *Strand* and *The Penny Dreadful*. He reckons that this will help both magazines to increase their sales as the subscribers to the *Strand* then purchase *The Penny Dreadful* to read the next instalment, and our readers do the same in return."

"Ahem."

At the sound of Mr Wigram clearing his throat, all eyes turned towards him as the elderly lawyer rose from his desk at the rear of the office.

"It does seem as though Mr Doyle's proposal might have some pecuniary benefits, Penelope. Perhaps we shouldn't dismiss it out of hand."

Meeting her guardian's gaze, Penny slowly nodded her agreement.

"It seems as though the Black Crow will take flight in a new adventure," she declared. "One where he will match his wits against the great detective, Sherlock Holmes."

"Bravo!"

As Alfie clapped his hands together in delight, Penny turned her attention to Monty again.

"But before you depart for Esher, we must discuss some initial ideas for the story. You must convince Conan Doyle that the thoughts of Montgomery Flinch are yours alone. We cannot risk our secret being discovered."

"Have no fear, Penelope," Monty replied. He gestured towards the books lining the shelves behind him, leather-bound volumes of *The Collected Tales of Montgomery Flinch*. "I have played this role for so long that half the time even I believe that I have written these stories. There is no chance of Arthur discovering the secret that we share."

The sudden rap of the door knocker punctuated the end of Monty's sentence. As Penny's gaze flicked to the door, the knocker rapped again, even louder this time.

"Keep your hair on," Alfie muttered, hurrying to the door with Monty's bat still in his grasp. As he opened it, the door knocker clanked back against its plate.

On the doorstep, a tall man in a shabby-looking suit glared back at Alfie. His dark eyes were set in a weasel-faced frame; his sallow complexion was more suited to the darkness than the bright light of day. The man was flanked by two police constables: the first a stocky, heavyset fellow who had the strap of his helmet pulled tight beneath his chin, as if to keep the few brains he looked like possessing safely secured, whilst his younger companion cast a nervous glance over Alfie's shoulder, his fingers fidgeting above the pocket where his truncheon was concealed.

Alfie slipped the cricket bat behind his back, a guilty blush colouring his cheeks, although for what crime he had no idea.

"Can I help you, sir?" he stuttered.

"I am here to see Montgomery Flinch," the man replied in a low voice, pushing past Alfie with a shove. "I have a warrant for his arrest."

V

"What on earth is the meaning of this?" Mr Wigram demanded, looking up in alarm as Alfie staggered backwards.

Ignoring his protest, the man strode into the heart of the office, casting his gaze around its interior with a practised air. He sniffed as his eyes fell on Monty, the actor still sitting behind Penelope's desk. The confident smile that had filled Monty's face only moments before was now beginning to curdle slightly at the corners. Penny looked on with concern as the two police constables lumbered across the threshold too, handcuffs clinking from where they hung on their leather belts.

"I'll ask you again," said Wigram, raising his voice to a querulous pitch. "Who are you, sir, and what business do you have here?"

Keeping his eyes fixed on Monty, the man sniffed again as he gave his reply.

"I am Inspector Drake of the Metropolitan

Police, and my business here is of a most serious nature."

Penelope paled at the inspector's remarks. The eventuality she had long feared must have finally come to pass. Somehow, someone must have uncovered Montgomery Flinch's secret, and now they would have to pay the price for their lies. Her mind filled with dark imaginings of the charges the police could bring: fraud, conspiracy, deception...

If her identity as the true face of the Master of the Macabre was revealed, Montgomery Flinch's reputation would be ruined and the renewed fortunes of *The Penny Dreadful* cast down with it too.

Blithely unaware of Penelope's fears, Monty greeted the detective with a grin.

"Ah, Inspector, welcome to *The Penny Dreadful*," he said, rising from his chair to offer his hand. "I will be delighted to help you with whatever matter is troubling your detectives, but are you sure that you haven't confused me with my good friend, Arthur Conan Doyle? He is, after all, the creator of the famous Sherlock Holmes, whereas my tales tend to be preoccupied with events of a more unearthly nature."

Inspector Drake stared down at Monty's outstretched hand with disdain.

"No," he replied with a shake of his head. "You're the man that I'm after."

"He's not here to ask your advice, Monty," Alfie called out, still rubbing his shoulder where the burly policeman had brushed past him. "He says he has a warrant for your arrest."

The colour drained from Monty's cheeks, but Alfie's warning had come too late as, with a brief nod of his head, Drake gestured to the nearer of the two constables. Acting swiftly, the man promptly clapped his handcuffs around Monty's outstretched wrist.

"What is the meaning of this effrontery?" Monty spluttered, staring down at the handcuffs in disbelief as the policeman twisted his wrist to secure the other hand inside. "This is preposterous! Do you not know who I am?"

Watching with a growing sense of horror, Penelope's heart raced in anticipation of the inspector's reply.

"I know exactly who you are, Mr Flinch," Drake said as the police constable roughly shoved Monty back into his seat. "Or should I call you the Black Crow?"

Penny gasped in surprise, the sound of this drawing the inspector's suspicious gaze.

"And who exactly are you, miss?"

For a moment, Penelope was lost for words, her thoughts a swirl of confusion at what she had just heard. The Black Crow was the villain from a story, not some real-life criminal. Surely this detective wasn't so simple-minded that he couldn't tell the difference between a fictional character and its creator. But inside her confusion, a seed of hope grew too. If the inspector didn't know who she was, then perhaps Montgomery Flinch's secret was still safe after all. She needed to find out what was really going on here.

Smoothing the pleats on her skirt, Penelope met the inspector's gaze with a simpering smile.

"I'm Miss Penelope Tredwell," she replied primly. "Montgomery Flinch is my uncle and I can assure you, inspector, that he is an innocent man. This must all be some terrible misunderstanding."

"Quite right," Monty grunted as he glared up at them from the chair. "What kind of cock-and-bull crime are you accusing me of anyway? If this is anything to do with my bar tab at the Athenaeum, then I assure you it is my intention to pay the bill in full."

Peering out from his sharp face, Drake's dark eyes flashed in anger.

"Do not mock me, Mr Flinch," he said in a warning tone. "You know full well the treasonous crime of which you stand accused: the theft of the Crown Jewels from the Tower of London itself."

Monty laughed in disbelief.

"But that's just a story," he cried. "You can't arrest me for writing about a fictional crime!"

Drawing himself up to his full height, Drake towered over Monty as the actor shrank back into his seat. The detective leaned forward until his face was only inches away from Monty's own.

"You might think you're clever, Mr Flinch," he hissed, "hiding your crime in plain sight, but your arrogance will be your downfall. Now tell me, where have you hidden the King's crown?"

For a moment there was silence, and then Alfie's voice piped up from the door.

"But surely if the Crown Jewels had been stolen it would be all over the newspapers by now? After all, the King's got to use his crown for his coronation next week."

"And that is why there has been no report of this crime," Inspector Drake replied, keeping his gaze fixed on Monty's face as he watched a bead of sweat slide down his brow. "If news of the theft of the Crown Jewels was to get out, there would be uproar: questions in the House, protests in the streets, the police and army pilloried for our failure to protect the King's crown. How could the coronation go ahead in such circumstances?" He leaned in even closer. "Now, tell me, Mr Flinch, how exactly did you think you would get away with bragging about your crime in the pages of *The Penny Dreadful*?"

As Monty squirmed in his seat, Penny stepped into the breach. Tapping the detective on his shoulder, she fixed her face in a disarmingly attentive expression.

"Excuse me, inspector, but if the Crown Jewels have been stolen as you say, why on earth do you believe that my uncle is responsible? Surely the more logical explanation is a copycat crime. Some enterprising thief must have taken inspiration from my uncle's story and then used its plot to enact their own audacious crime."

Inspector Drake returned Penny's gaze with a condescending stare.

"That would be the more logical explanation, Miss Tredwell," he replied. "And rest assured, the Metropolitan Police would have pursued such an obvious theory if it wasn't for one fatal flaw – the theft of the Crown Jewels took place some five weeks before your uncle's story was published."

The detective turned back to face Monty, the expression on his face grim.

"The Tower of London is a fortress. The Crown Jewels themselves are guarded in its highest tower, hidden behind locked doors and stone walls twenty feet thick. It is the most impregnable building in the whole of the British Empire, but the Keeper of the Keys swears that he saw the hooded figure of the Black Crow walk through its walls without a care."

Behind Drake, the taller of the two police constables twitched, his eyes fixed on Monty's outstretched wrists as if fearful that he would suddenly slip free from his handcuffs just like Harry Houdini. From the other side of the desk, Penelope listened with a growing sense of dread as the inspector continued to speak.

"Now, ordinarily I would have taken such a statement with a large pinch of salt and put down this tale of a phantom thief to nothing more than the fevered imaginings of an old soldier rather too fond of his rum. But when dozens of eyewitnesses say that they saw the exact same sight then I start to wonder myself. Especially when I then read every detail of the crime they described in the pages of your magazine." He grabbed hold of Monty's shirt collar, pulling the actor's face close to his own. "How on earth did you achieve such a feat, Flinch? And what have you done with the Crown Jewels?"

Monty whimpered in fear. "I don't know what you are talking about." His eyes darted past Drake's shoulder, seeking out Penny with a plaintive stare. "Tell him, Penelope."

Penny stood there speechless, the inspector's accusation still ringing in her ears: the Crown Jewels stolen by the hand of the Black Crow. It was impossible, but then with a sudden lurch of understanding she realised that it must be true. The letter...

The image of the envelope addressed to Montgomery Flinch sprang into her mind, an illustration of a black crow marking its seal. This had given her the name of her villain, whilst the anonymous letter inside had been the spark for her story of *The Thief Who Wasn't There*. The first lines of this letter now echoed mockingly in her mind. *You are the only man in London I can trust with this confession. The newspapers stay silent, but I know The Penny Dreadful will not fear to reveal the truth of this conspiracy.*

Penelope's gaze flicked to the piles of unopened envelopes still littering Alfie's desk. At the time, she had thought this strange letter was just like all the rest: a flight of fictional fancy concocted by one of their readers, but now she could see the truth in its lines – the anonymous thief using *The Penny Dreadful* to mock his pursuers.

"Penelope, please!"

She stared back into Monty's pleading eyes, as next to him the plainclothes detective turned towards her with a suspicious stare. Her thoughts raced, trying to find a way out of this predicament. Even if she told Inspector Drake the truth, there was no guarantee that he would believe her. The only evidence she had to prove that Montgomery Flinch wasn't behind the theft of the Crown Jewels was one anonymous letter. No name, no address, no lead to follow – Drake would just think that her story was some desperate ruse to clear her "uncle's" name.

And what's more, if she did reveal the letter, then she dreaded to think of the further questions it would bring. Why had Montgomery Flinch chosen this plot to mark his return to the literary world? What other inspiration had fed his invention of the villainous Black Crow? And how come his "niece" knew more about his stories than the man himself? If she told the truth, she ran the risk of exposing them all.

As if growing weary of waiting for her reply, Drake gave a dismissive grunt. With a nod of his head, he gestured to the two constables who lumbered forward to haul Monty to his feet.

"We're wasting our time here," he snapped. "Let's see if we can get some more sense out of you after you've spent a night in the cells."

The two policemen began to drag Monty towards the door, the actor spluttering in protest as his cricket shoes scraped against the dusty floorboards.

"This is ridiculous! Unhand me at once!" Glancing back wildly, he caught Penny's gaze again. "You have to tell them the truth, Penelope!"

With these last words, she felt Inspector Drake's eyes turn towards her again, the detective's nose twitching at this mention of the truth. She stood there frozen, Montgomery Flinch's fate in her hands. Deep down, she knew the only chance she had of clearing Monty's name was to find out the truth herself. She would have to track down the author of the anonymous letter and unmask this real-life Black Crow. But first she had to make sure Monty didn't spill any of the secrets that they shared.

With an anguished wail, she rushed towards

him, flinging herself between the two policemen and wrapping her arms around Monty's neck.

"I won't let them take you, Uncle," she cried with a snivelling sob. "Your only crime is to be touched by clairvoyance. It's just as Mama says, you must have the gift of second sight if these stories that you write are so close to the truth. How else could you have known about this terrible crime?"

Leaning closer, Penny dropped her voice to a low whisper, pressing her mouth to Monty's ear.

"You have to keep quiet, for all our sakes. If Inspector Drake finds out that your real name is Monty Maples, you'll be facing charges of fraud, deception and conspiracy instead."

Monty's eyes grew wide as he realised he was caught on the horns of a dilemma. There was no way of revealing the truth without facing the consequences that this would bring. As the younger police constable tried to peel Penelope off Monty like some kind of limpet suffragette, she clung even closer still.

"I will make sure that Mr Wigram gets this ridiculous case dismissed," Penny hissed. "But for now you must convince Inspector Drake that you really are Montgomery Flinch, not some imposter. That would only make things worse."

With a trembling nod, Monty signalled to her that he understood.

"Get that girl off him," Drake barked.

Penny felt a pair of bear-like arms wrap themselves around her waist, the sudden rough embrace holding her more tightly than any corset. As she gasped in surprise, the second burly policeman lifted her off her feet, her arms flailing free as he hauled her across the office before dumping her down into the chair that Monty had just vacated.

"Sit still," he growled.

He turned back to where his fellow constable had seized hold of Monty again, the actor's face pulled in a pained grimace as the handcuffs chafed at his wrists. Winded, Penelope glowered from the depths of her chair, desperately praying that Monty would heed her warning.

Inspector Drake stepped forward, meeting Penny's defiant gaze with a glare.

"Let us have no more of this unseemly behaviour, Miss Tredwell. I appreciate your feelings of family loyalty, but your uncle is accused of a treasonous crime. You must not reveal a word of what you have learned today. Otherwise I will have no choice but to take you into custody as well."

Leaving this threat hanging in the air, Drake turned and, with a snap of his fingers, pointed the way to the door. Following his command, the two police constables dragged Monty forward again, his howls of protest now turned to wails of despair.

Then from the rear of the office came the sound of a cough. Buttoning up his grey morning coat, Mr Wigram stepped out of the shadows.

"As Mr Flinch's lawyer, I will, of course, be accompanying him to the police station. If you are going to persist with these outrageous allegations, then I insist that you allow my client the privilege of legal counsel."

Inspector Drake cast the elderly lawyer an exasperated stare.

"The more the merrier," he sniffed. He reached inside his pocket to pull out a crumpled envelope, presenting this to Wigram with a thin-lipped smile. "And as a policeman, I expect you to ensure that *The Penny Dreadful* obeys the laws of the land."

Opening the envelope, Mr Wigram paled as he read the letter inside. As the two police constables pushed Monty out through the front door of the office, Inspector Drake turned to follow them, leaving Wigram standing there alone.

"What is it?" Penelope asked. Leaving her chair, she hurried to her guardian's side.

With a shake of his head, Wigram thrust the letter into her hands.

"The end," he replied grimly. "They're closing the magazine down."

Penny stared down at the letter in disbelief, recognising the royal seal above the copperplate script.

BY ORDER OF THE LORD CHAMBERLAIN, NOTICE IS HEREBY SERVED UPON THE PROPRIETORS OF THE PENNY DREADFUL MAGAZINE THAT THIS PERIODICAL SHOULD CEASE PUBLICATION FORTHWITH. ALL EXISTING COPIES OF THE JULY 1902 EDITION SHOULD BE DESTROYED, AND ANY MATERIALS USED FOR THE PREPARATION OF THIS EDITION SURRENDERED TO THE AUTHORITIES WITHOUT DELAY. FAILURE TO COMPLY WITH THIS ROYAL DECREE WILL RESULT IN IMMEDIATE IMPRISONMENT.

"They can't do this," she cried, indignation shining in her eyes.

From the doorway, the gruff voice of Inspector Drake gave his reply.

"They can and they have," he growled. "The King's coronation will take place in five days' time. If Montgomery Flinch has planned any further treasonous crimes, the public will not learn of them from the pages of his magazine. You shut it down – now!"

With this final warning delivered, Drake marched out of the door. As it slammed shut behind him, Penny could still hear Monty's anguished cries as the policemen bundled him down the stone steps.

Her guardian clasped her hands in his own.

"You must return home at once, Penelope; there's nothing more you can do here. I will do my best to facilitate Mr Maples' release."

Glancing back over his shoulder, the lawyer lowered his voice to a whisper.

"There is danger here. Somehow this story of yours has unleashed forces that I do not understand. Please keep yourself safe until my return."

As he hurried out of the door in pursuit of Inspector Drake, Penny stared down at the letter again. Her mind whirled with unanswered questions, the mystery growing with every second that passed. The Crown Jewels stolen, Monty arrested, *The Penny Dreadful* put out of business by royal decree.

When she looked up again, Alfie's worried face was staring back at her; the two of them were now alone in the office. There was a long moment of silence before Alfie finally spoke.

"What do we do now?" he asked.

Her guardian's words of warning echoed at the back of her mind. *There is danger here.* Ignoring this, Penelope set her face in a determined manner, lips pursed as she reached for her parasol that was hanging from the coat stand.

"We find out who has really stolen the Crown Jewels," she replied, striding briskly towards the door as Alfie hurried to grab his coat. "I think we should start with a spot of sightseeing at the Tower."

VI

The afternoon sun hung high in the sky, bathing the Tower in a golden light. Its turrets and ramparts glistened like a grey stone forest, the frowning battlements flanked by a series of smaller towers, stretching along the riverbank. Beneath Tower Bridge, the muddy waters of the Thames were churned by paddles and oars, tiny skiffs and pleasure barges eddying in the swell of the steamers seeking a berth at St Katharine Docks.

Penny and Alfie strolled along Tower Wharf, the trees shading the promenade offering them some welcome relief from the heat of the day. Blossom hung from every branch, and petals lay scattered across the cobblestones. It was as if nature itself was trying to compete with the brightly coloured bunting draped between the street lamps. Along the walkway, sightseers mingled with river workers, leisurely gaits and ruddy faces with heads held high replacing the stooping shoulders and anxious looks that were more usually seen in a London crowd. They were nearing the south-west corner of the castle now, the throngs of people growing thicker as Penny and Alfie approached the entrance to the Tower itself.

"So what are we going to do when we get inside?" Alfie asked, a nervous smile pinching his features. "If we ask to see where the Crown Jewels were stolen, they'll probably lock us up in the Tower too."

Penelope shook her head.

"There must be a clue that the police have missed." She stared up at the imposing keep. "It's ridiculous to think that a thief could walk through these walls and stroll off with the Crown Jewels tucked in their pocket. This isn't a story."

Alfie arched an eyebrow, but seeing the frown on Penny's face wisely kept his own counsel.

They were nearing the front of the crowd now, dozens of people huddled outside the squat towers that stood guard at the entrance. But beneath the stonework of the royal crest, the huge oak doors were bolted, and on the sign where the entrance prices were posted, a single word was written:

CLOSED

As the milling tourists slowly turned away, Penelope overheard a dapper gentleman as he turned to his companion. "They say it's closed for the King's coronation," he brayed. "They must all be busy polishing his crown ready for the big day."

As the lady on his arm laughed coquettishly, Alfie shot Penny a knowing glance.

"Talk about closing the stable door after the horse has bolted," he muttered.

Beyond the Spur Gate, Penelope could see the Bell and Byward Towers, their impregnable walls silently mocking her with their secrets. Her gaze returned to the locked gates, a lone soldier standing sentry there. There was no way she could slip past him to sneak inside the Tower. Still, if she couldn't inspect the scene of the crime, perhaps there was another way she could find the answers she was searching for.

She thought back to what Inspector Drake had told them. The detective had mentioned numerous eyewitnesses, but only one by name: the Keeper of the Keys. From her study of the pages of *The Navy & Army Illustrated* magazine, she had learned that the present Keeper of the Keys was one Sergeant Major Thomas Middleton, the Chief Warder of the Tower. It was time to find out if he had really seen the hooded figure of the Black Crow walk through these walls.

"Wait here," she told Alfie.

Without giving him the chance to reply, Penny set off at a brisk pace, heading directly for the Tower Warder. As she approached, the old soldier's gaze stayed fixed firmly ahead, even as the dainty clatter of Penelope's heels on the cobblestones announced her arrival. She stared up at the grizzled veteran, his dark-blue tunic and trousers edged with scarlet bands and his broad chest covered in medals. Before taking up the duties of a Tower Warder, these soldiers had served the Empire with distinction, a billet at the Tower their just reward on retirement from active service.

Penelope cleared her throat to try to attract the guard's attention.

"Excuse me, sir," she began.

From beneath the broad brim of his black velvet hat, the warder looked down at Penelope with a flinty stare.

"Can I help you, miss?"

"I need to speak to the Chief Warder of the Tower," she replied. "It is a matter of great urgency."

The yeoman warder shook his head.

"That's quite out of the question, miss. Sergeant Major Middleton is not on duty at the moment, but if you leave your message with me, I will ensure that it is delivered without delay on his return."

Thinking fast, Penny crumpled her features into a crestfallen expression.

"But Mother said I was to speak only to Uncle Thomas – I mean Sergeant Major Middleton.

This is a family matter. The doctor doesn't think Mama will last another night, and she dearly wishes to speak to her eldest brother one last time before she passes over to the other side."

The warder shifted uncomfortably in his shoes. Rules and regulations were one thing, but he didn't want to deny a dying woman's wish. Penelope's barefaced lie was having the desired effect.

"You cannot come inside, miss," he said, leaning closer as if he was fearful of being overheard. "No visitors allowed within the bounds of the Tower, by order of the King. But if you want to find Sergeant Major Middleton, you might try your luck at The Anchor Tap." With a tilt of his head, he nodded towards the river. Penelope followed the direction of his gaze until her eyes alighted upon the Anchor Brewery sitting on the south bank, its high chimney belching a trail of contented smoke into the pale-blue sky.

With a smile of thanks, Penelope turned to leave, pleased that she had managed to hoodwink the warder.

"Be careful, miss," the guard called out as she began to walk back to where Alfie was waiting. "The Anchor Tap is no place for a young lady like you."

VII

As she stood on the threshold of the public house, Penelope could see that the old soldier had been telling the truth. Outside the sun was still high in the sky, the summer afternoon slowly idling its way towards evening, but here inside the tavern, darkness reigned. Dark-oak walls framed a cramped public bar, its woodwork stained almost black where it could be glimpsed amidst a press of elbows.

Wiping a pint glass with the hem of her pinafore, a sour-faced barmaid was serving a gaggle of burly dockworkers, their crude attempts to coax a smile rousing the pub with their laughter. In the corner of the bar, an old soldier banged out a regimental tune on an upright piano, a young woman in a low-cut French dress perched on his lap. As the soldier reached the chorus, she joined in with his singing, her tuneless screech causing Penny to wince in discomfort. The revels seemed more suited to a Friday night free-and-easy than a sunny Tuesday afternoon.

As the tavern door closed behind Penelope, she became uncomfortably aware of the gazes now turned in her direction. With Alfie standing protectively by her side, she felt eyes crawling over every inch of her outfit, inspecting the finery of its embroidery and the shine of her shoes. It was clear by the sneers that this wasn't a place where she was welcome.

"Are you sure this is a good idea?" Alfie murmured.

Penny held her head high. With Monty for the moment keeping his counsel behind the bars of New Scotland Yard, it was time for her to find the man who might hold the key to his freedom. Surveying the bar, she couldn't see any sign of a face that matched the portrait of Sergeant Major Middleton she had seen in the pages of *The Navy & Army Illustrated* magazine. But, to the left of the bar, she spied an open door.

"We have to find the Keeper of the Keys," she replied, linking her arm with Alfie's. "Let's try this way."

The two of them negotiated their way past the bar, ignoring the muttered comments from the men propped up there. Through the door, she could see further rooms stretching back into the pub; these snug dens were populated by those drinkers who wanted to conduct their business away from prying eyes. And there, at a table in the corner, she saw the figure of a man sitting staring into the bottom of a half-empty glass. Penelope recognised his long bushy beard from the portrait she had seen. Sergeant Major Thomas Middleton – the Chief Warder of the Tower of London and the Keeper of the Keys. Beneath an army greatcoat, the old soldier's shoulders were hunched, his face turned away from the dull light spilling in from the smoked-glass windows.

"That's him," she murmured, nudging Alfie as they stepped inside the warren-like room. The other tables in the snug were filled with numerous rough-looking coves: coal-whippers, stave porters, lumpers and labourers. Calloused hands cradled glasses as the men cast them both suspicious glances. With low mutters following their every step, Penny led the way to Middleton's table, the floorboards beneath her feet sticky with spilled drinks and other dubious stains.

As Alfie fidgeted nervously by her side, Penelope took this opportunity to take a closer look at the Chief Warder. Middleton's head was still bowed, his gaze seemingly fixed to the bottom of his glass. His army portrait had shown a distinguished-looking man, his long beard silvered with age, but the hunched figure in front of her seemed somehow broken. He appeared unaware of their presence, the huddle of empty glasses littering the small table a measure of how long he had been here.

Endeavouring to gain his attention, Penelope cleared her throat.

"Excuse me, Sergeant Major Middleton?"

The old soldier lifted his head, staring up at her with flint-grey eyes. His face was ghastly pale, his expression haggard and drawn as if nursing some unspeakable suffering. Penelope had seen this expression before, recognising the distant stare from the faces of the soldiers her father had served with in British India. The men who had fought in the North-West Frontier Uprising, seen women and children dragged from their beds and murdered by the marauding tribesmen. It was the face of a man who had seen too much.

Penelope frowned, unnerved by the soldier's silence. According to his regimental record, Sergeant Major Middleton hadn't seen active service for more than a decade. His comfortable billet at the Tower of London was a far cry from his days fighting in the Indian Mutiny. A ghost who walked through walls, that's what Drake said the Keeper of the Keys had seen, but how could that be? She had to find out exactly what Middleton had witnessed. Penny glanced down again at the empty glasses. *In vino veritas*, she prayed.

"Do I know you, miss?" The sudden sound of Middleton's voice made Penny's heart skip a beat. His quavering tone seemed strained, as if he was in pain. "I have come here to find some peace, not be lectured about scripture and the merits of temperance."

Penny stared back at him in confusion before the realisation slowly dawned. Middleton must have mistaken her for a member of the British Women's Temperance Association: the do-gooders who visited taverns encouraging drinkers to seek salvation in the arms of the Lord and mend their ways at last.

"No, sir, you are mistaken," Penelope began and then paused to try to gather her thoughts. What exactly was she going to tell him? She could hardly say that she had heard he had seen a ghost steal the Crown Jewels. She thought back to what she had learned from the Chief Warder's regimental record: tours of duty in India, Afghanistan and the Nile; Middleton had even served on the North-West Frontier, just like her father...

Unbidden, the image of her father's face crept into her mind, his dark whiskers neatly trimmed in the military style. She could picture him in his officer's uniform, his arm draped around her mother's elegant shoulders as the regimental photographer captured their portrait. She recalled the yellowish tint of the telegram that brought her news of their deaths, her father and mother both murdered in the bloody North-West Frontier Uprising. Her heart ached, the pain of her loss undimmed by the passing of the years.

"Then what is your business here?" the old soldier demanded, his trembling fingers clinging to his pint glass as if seeking sanctuary there. "Can you not leave me in peace?"

Penny racked her mind, desperately seeking an answer that would make Sergeant Major Middleton take her into his trust. Apart from his military medals, *The Penny Dreadful* was all she had left of her father now. If finding out exactly what Middleton had seen could somehow help her save the magazine, then she was prepared to say almost anything – even lie if that would bring her closer to the truth.

Suddenly in her mind, Penny heard the echo of her father's voice. She could picture him sitting in the chair next to her bed, soft shadows falling across his face as he read to her from the book of poetry in his hand, so different from the tales of mystery and adventure that they usually shared.

"A lie which is all a lie may be met and fought with outright, but a lie which is part a truth is a harder matter to fight."

In her father's words, Penelope suddenly realised how she might gain Middleton's trust: a lie wrapped in the truth. There was one thing that Sergeant Major Middleton and her father both shared...

"My father said I should find you, sir," she said, primly seating herself on one of the vacant chairs at the table. "He was under your command on the North-West Frontier. He told me you were the truest officer he ever had the privilege of serving with."

As Alfie joined them at the table, Middleton's stare softened a little, this mention of an old army comrade taking his thoughts back to simpler times.

"The Gordon Highlanders," he murmured. "Finest men I have ever known."

His gaze focused on Penelope again.

"What did you say your father's name was, miss?"

"Tredwell," Penny replied, her eyes glistening in the gloom of the snug. "His name was Lieutenant Archibald Tredwell."

As the old soldier scratched at his prodigious beard, trying to place the name through an alcoholic fug, Penelope fought back her own tears. Since her parents' funeral all those years ago, Penny hadn't allowed herself to grieve. Instead she had poured out her misery into the pages of *The Penny Dreadful*. Now she had to make sure that her father's magazine lived on in tribute to his memory.

"I'm afraid I don't recall a Lieutenant Tredwell," Middleton finally replied, the words half slurred into the depths of his glass as he took a final swig. "Tell your father that he must have mistaken me for another man."

Wiping a tear from the corner of her eye, Penny

slowly shook her head.

"I can't do that, sir," she said, her voice cracking a little. "My father has been dead for the past five years."

A baffled look stole across the old soldier's features.

"I'm terribly sorry," he began, bowing his head in sympathy. "But how then could your father have told you to find me?"

On the wall of the snug, a tattered poster gave Penelope her answer.

THE INDESCRIBABLE PHENOMENON

MISS EUSAPIA PALLADINO

is in London, and will hold

PUBLIC SEANCES

....

EVERY EVENING, EXCEPT SUNDAY
AT BATTERSEA SPIRITUALIST CHURCH

Open to all persons who desire to hear the spirits talk

....

TICKETS: 2s 6d, ADMITTING GENTLEMAN AND LADY

"I've seen her, sir," Penelope replied, gesturing over Middleton's shoulder to the poster behind him. "Miss Palladino – the medium. She told me that my father had a message for me – a message from the other side." Penny stumbled over her words, her mind spinning the lie almost as quickly as she could speak it. "He told me that I needed to seek out Sergeant Major Middleton, the man who tried to save his life back at the Malakand Pass. He said that he owed you a debt of thanks and I now had to help you in your hour of need."

Beneath his silvering thatch of hair, Middleton's brow furrowed with anxious thought.

"My hour of need," he murmured. "What exactly do you mean?"

Penelope fixed him with a sympathetic stare.

"He said you were haunted by a ghost, sir – a ghost who could walk through walls."

The blood drained from Middleton's face, his deathly-pale features crumpling in horror.

"My God," he breathed. "You know about the spectre who stole the Crown Jewels."

His eyes darted past Penelope's face, casting a furtive glance around the room as if fearful of who might have overheard him. Then the old solider gestured for Penny to come closer, leaning forward himself until the distance between them was only a matter of inches.

Penelope wrinkled her nose as she smelled the stale stench of ale on his breath, but as Middleton began to speak again, his voice a low whisper, all thoughts of this disappeared as she listened to him recount what had happened on that fateful night.

"It was the night of the tenth of May, an ordinary night just like any other, as I carried out my duties at the Tower. The gates were locked, as they always are, at eight minutes to eleven. First the Middle and the Byward Towers, then as I walked across the cobbles beneath the Bloody Tower I caught my first glimpse of him. At first I thought he was just a waif and stray who had somehow got lost in the Tower, but then when I stepped forward to challenge him, I saw his face beneath his scarf..."

Middleton's voice trailed into silence, his eyes glazing over as he relived that terrible moment again.

Penelope leaned forward, eager to find out more. "What did you see?" she asked.

"His face," Middleton murmured, his distant gaze staring into the gloom. "It glowed."

Seated next to her, Penny heard Alfie stifle a chuckle and she shot him a warning glance. Middleton, however, didn't even show that he'd heard this, his voice a cracked whisper as he continued to speak.

"As a child I'd heard stories about the radiant boys – glowing ghosts that told of disasters to come. My grandmother used to say they were angels of death, and any man who saw them was destined to die."

Radiant boys... The echo of these words rang in Penny's mind. She had heard this somewhere before. As she groped for the answer, Sergeant Major Middleton slowly pulled up the sleeve of his greatcoat, presenting his right arm to Penelope. She saw with a shudder the burn that covered his forearm: the shape of five fingers pressed against puckered flesh, the skin beneath a brilliant red.

"I felt his touch, Miss Tredwell, and it wasn't the touch of a mortal man. It still burns, and I fear that this wound will be the death of me. You cannot help me now. I have failed the King and the shame will follow me to an early grave."

With a pained grimace, Middleton pulled back his sleeve, hiding the burn once more. "Leave me now," he said, a note of command returning to the old soldier's voice. "I want to be left in peace with my sins."

Penelope opened her mouth to ask another question, but before she could speak, she felt Alfie rest his hand on her shoulder.

"We should leave now," he said, his face almost as pale as the soldier's. Behind him, Penny could see the huddle of labourers rising from their chairs, angry stares darting in their direction. Leaving Sergeant Major Middleton staring into the bottom of his empty glass, Penny and Alfie hurried for the door.

"So what now?" Alfie asked once they were

safely outside the tavern, the two of them hastening up Horselydown Lane. "We still don't know who might have stolen the Crown Jewels."

Blinking in the late afternoon sunlight, Penelope shaded her eyes with her hand. In her mind, she could still see the image of the burn seared across the old soldier's skin, the impossible echo of his words haunting her still. *Glowing ghosts... Angels of death... The radiant boys...* Her mind whirred, the words finally clicking into place. She now knew where she had heard this before. In the offices of *The Penny Dreadful*, scattered amidst the countless competition entries, she remembered the torn newspaper clippings reporting sightings of strange wraiths and radiant boys haunting the streets of London.

She turned back towards Alfie. "Oh, but we do," she replied with a smile. "We're looking for the radiant boys."

VIII

Penelope studied the newspapers fanned out across the reading-room table in front of her: *The Times*, *The Morning Post*, *The Illustrated London News* and countless more. Newsprint stained her fingertips as she leafed through the pages of the *Evening Standard*. Beneath its masthead, the date Monday, May 12, 1902 could be read. Two days after Sergeant Major Middleton said the Crown Jewels had been stolen.

Penny's eyes scanned the rows of columns, flicking past each article and report in turn, searching for the clue that would bring her one step closer to solving this mystery. Of course, there was no mention of the theft of the Crown Jewels in any of the newspapers she had read; Inspector Drake and his men had made sure of that. No, Penelope was searching for a different sort of story.

Her gaze snagged on a brief article tucked away

at the bottom of page thirteen, its headline telling her that she had found her lead at last.

A RADIANT BOY HAUNTS BLACKFRIARS

◆

The neighbourhood of Ludgate Hill has been thrown into a state of extraordinary excitement by the rumour that a supernatural apparition has been sighted. On Saturday night, Henry Chappell, a respectable-looking man, was returning to his lodgings at 6 Carter Lane, Blackfriars, when he reportedly saw an apparition walking through the wall of the Old Bell Tavern. Several other revellers frequenting the tavern attested to witnessing the same, with one even describing how he pursued the apparition along Ludgate Hill where the insubstantial form disappeared without a trace. The description of the spectre given by each of the witnesses is the same – a young man with glowing features dressed in a long flowing coat.

A small smile of satisfaction played around Penelope's lips. This was the very same story she had first seen clipped from the pages of this newspaper and posted to her at *The Penny Dreadful*. At the time she had dismissed it as yet another half-baked competition entry, the person who sent it seemingly believing that Montgomery Flinch could conjure up a tale of the macabre from such meagre fare. Her gaze settled again on the headline:

A RADIANT BOY HAUNTS BLACKFRIARS

◆

The few scant details reported here seemed to match the description that Sergeant Major Middleton had given her exactly: a young man with glowing features, dressed in a long flowing coat; a boy who could walk through walls.

The story of *The Thief Who Wasn't There* had been here all along, she just hadn't realised it. This must be the man, if it was a man, who had stolen the Crown Jewels.

Taking a careful note of where the sighting had been reported, Penny pushed the newspaper to one side. Beneath this lay a map of London, the city's streets and parks covering most of the table. Seated around her, the other library patrons muttered reprovingly as the rustle of papers disturbed their peace. Ignoring this, Penelope searched out Blackfriars on the map, marking the exact spot with a cross and against this noting the date and time when the sighting had been reported. Clearing the rest of the newspapers out of the way, she studied the map with a sigh.

The map showed the whole of London pitted

with the marks Penelope had made. From Mayfair to Sloane Square, South Kensington to the Elephant and Castle, a graveyard of crosses were scattered across the city. No rhyme and reason, it seemed, to where the ghost of the radiant boy had been seen. These sightings didn't just date from the night of the tenth of May. Indeed, the reports of strange glowing figures seemed to have plagued the city for the past month, with light-hearted articles detailing ghostly sightings tucked away under News in Brief. But if anyone took the trouble of joining the dots, it looked like an invasion of the dead...

A sudden gleam of realisation shone in Penelope's pale-green eyes, the idea coming to her in an instant. That's what she had to do. Reaching beneath her chair, she lifted her valise up on to the table, unfastening its clasp with a satisfying click. As a chorus of tuts sounded again, Penny drew out a ruler from her bag and placed this on the map. Moving her case to one side, she began to draw a series of lines between each of the ink crosses she had already marked on the map, working through these in order to trace the paths that the ghostly figure must have taken as he slipped through the streets of the city.

Gradually, a pattern began to emerge as the lines meandered through Westminster, Whitehall and the Mall. By tracing each night's journey back to its earliest sighting, the lines all seemed to converge on a single spot – a property near the corner of Carlton House Terrace in the heart of St James's. Penelope frowned. What business could a ghost have in this fashionable street populated by lords, earls and ambassadors?

She glanced down at her watch. It was half past four. Alfie should be back from the printers now. Even though *The Penny Dreadful* had been banned from publication, there was still work to be done: printer's bills to pay, paper orders to cancel, the pulping of returns to oversee. In Wigram's absence as he tried to free Monty, Alfie had stepped into the breach, taking on the older man's duties as he and Penny fought to keep the magazine alive.

Folding up the map, Penelope placed it in her valise, snapping the clasp shut with a determined look. She would pick up Alfie on the way to Carlton House Terrace.

It was time to go ghost hunting.

Away from the din and bustle of traffic, Penny and Alfie hurried down Pall Mall. Garlands of flowers and strings of gaily coloured bunting criss-crossed the street; the coronation decorations hung resplendent between the grand palatial buildings. Beneath this finery, a stream of elegantly dressed men strolled down the pavement, hansom cabs dropping their occupants at the doors of one or other of the grand gentlemen's clubs that called this street their home. Passing by the classical columns of the United Service Club, Penelope turned left down Waterloo Place.

"So we're following in the footsteps of a ghost?" Alfie asked as he studied the oversized map flapping in his hands. Taking his arm, Penny steered him past the sneering glance of a well-heeled businessman, the pavement narrowing as they passed beneath the broad-leafed trees bordering the club's private garden.

"We're following in the footsteps of a thief," she corrected him. "I can't see what use a ghost would have for the Crown Jewels of Empire."

"Perhaps it's the ghost of Henry the Eighth?" Alfie suggested with a grin. "Come back from the grave to claim his crown."

Penelope shook her head as they crossed the road at the end of the avenue.

"I've never heard of a ghost whose touch could brand a living man," she said. "Not even the ghost of a king."

In his mind, Alfie saw the burn mark scorched across Middleton's arm, the memory of it sending a shiver down his spine.

Penelope came to a halt beneath the Duke of York's statue, its shadow lengthening as evening approached. Taking the map from Alfie, she studied the place where the lines converged. To her left she could see a grand terrace of white-stucco-fronted houses overlooking a private park. This was the street where the radiant boy's nightly journeys seemed to begin. Perhaps one of these houses held the key to unlocking this mystery.

With Alfie by her side, Penny started to walk along the terrace. The houses were set back behind wrought-iron railings. Corinthian columns buttressed sweeping balconies, each property reaching up for three storeys. Penelope gazed up in awe, her eyes searching for some kind of clue amid the grandeur. Then she spotted it, a nameplate fixed beside the front door of the second house on the left: *The Society for the Advancement of Science*. Her mind flicked back to the anonymous letter, her fingers twitching as she recollected the confession she had read. *You must believe me when I say I do not wish to do these things that they ask of me, but when that terrible fire races through my veins I am powerless to refuse. I am a living man, but these experiments are turning me into a ghost.* These experiments...

"This is the place," Penny murmured, staring up at the elegant façade. The high windows lay in darkness, blinds drawn to keep out the early-evening sun. "It's time to find the thief who wasn't there."

She climbed up the stone steps that led to the front door, Alfie following uneasily behind. He glanced nervously up at the grand portico.

"Are you just going to knock on the door?" he asked.

Penny shook her head, reaching up to the black ceramic bell push, set high on the wall.

"I think I'll try the doorbell."

In reply, a faint tinkling sound came from within. They waited, Alfie shuffling uncomfortably in his shoes as the seconds ticked by into minutes. The front door remained resolutely shut.

"Perhaps we should try the tradesmen's entrance," Alfie suggested.

With a nod of agreement, Penny followed him as they retraced their steps. Behind a small gate in the railings, a narrow flight of steps led the way below stairs. Reaching the bottom, Penelope wrinkled her nose in the gloom. To her right, beneath a recessed porch, stood the tradesmen's entrance, a sign fixed to the black-painted door proclaiming, "No hawkers or pedlars. All deliveries must be made between the hours of 8.00 a.m. and 6.00 p.m." A strange smell of chemicals hung in the air, the most likely source the four tall dustbins standing in the shadows near the door. Next to these bins, stacks of empty bottles and beakers were arranged with geometrical precision in open wooden cases. Penny's gaze ranged over the scene, taking this all in with a novelist's eye. If the radiant boy had come from this place, then the initial evidence seemed to suggest that there might be a scientific explanation for this rather than any supernatural cause.

As Alfie skulked in the shadows, Penny rang the bell next to the door. The clang of this sounded louder down here, but there still came no answering reply. It looked like the Society for the Advancement of Science had closed for the night.

"We'll have to come back during office hours," Alfie suggested, glancing down at his watch. "There's bound to be someone here then."

Disappointed, Penny looked down again at the map in her hand. Next to each of the ink crosses where she had recorded the sightings, she saw that every single one of these had occurred after dark. A slow smile of realisation crept across her lips. Of course, who had ever heard of a ghost who chose to walk in daylight?

"I think we should stay." She glanced around in the gloom, searching for a place where they could hide out of sight. "Let's wait to see what darkness brings."

IX

Penelope sniffed, a disdainful expression curling her lip. An unsavoury smell was emanating from the depths of the dustbins they were hiding behind, a strange brew of chemicals and decay. Beneath her feet she could feel a sticky residue clinging to the soles of her summer shoes and she tried not to think how much they had cost her from the Regent Street shop only weeks before. Peering past the stacks of wooden crates, she saw the door lay in darkness; still no sign of any shadowy comings or goings. She glanced down at her watch again. It was nearly ten.

Her thoughts turned to home. If Wigram had returned from the police station, he was sure to be worrying about her whereabouts now. Perhaps it was time to abandon this wild ghost chase and concentrate her energies on pursuing other ways of clearing Monty's name. With a sigh, she leaned against the wall of the building, almost ready to admit defeat. But then, through the cool brick, she felt a distant shudder, followed by an almost imperceptible whine at the very edge of her hearing.

Penny turned towards Alfie, her friend still skulking in the shadows.

"Did you hear that?" she asked.

Alfie's stomach rumbled in reply, the mutton pie he had consumed for lunch long forgotten.

"I'm sorry," he said, the darkness hiding his blushes. "I'm starving."

"I'm not talking about your stomach," Penny replied, pressing her ear against the wall. "Listen."

Alfie strained his ears, slowly nodding his head as he heard the same high-pitched whine.

"What is it?" he asked.

"I don't know," Penny said, keeping her voice low. "But it's coming from inside."

The two of them stood silent in the gloom, listening intently to try and discern what on earth was making this sound, when suddenly it ceased.

Alfie glanced towards Penny, her face still hidden in the shadows.

"If there's somebody working in there, perhaps we should knock on the door again."

He took half a step forward, but then Penny grabbed hold of his arm.

"Wait," she hissed, her eyes fixed on the door. "Look."

Following her gaze, Alfie froze in fear. In the

darkness, the shadows were moving. The door was still closed, but Penelope watched spellbound as a figure dressed in a long dark coat slowly emerged from the gloom. His face was swathed in a muffling scarf, a broad black cap pulled low over his eyes. But between the brim of his cap and the dark material of his scarf, Penny could just see the thin strip of skin around his eyes. It glowed.

She shrank back into the shadows, her hand clinging to Alfie's arm as her friend held his breath. With a swift glance around him, the radiant boy began to climb the steps that led to the street above, his footsteps silent against the stone.

"Shall we follow him?" Alfie whispered, his initial sense of alarm replaced with an eagerness to finally escape from their hiding space.

Penny was just about to agree to her friend's suggestion, when another movement in the shadows stilled her lips. From the darkness of the closed door, yet more figures were emerging. They seemed more like shadows than men; black greatcoats trailing through the gloom as each figure climbed towards the darkness of the street. Every face was masked by the same swathes of dark material, the scarves covering their features almost completely. As her heart thumped in her chest, Penny prayed that none of these radiant boys would glance towards the place where they were hiding. She felt Alfie's hand steal into her own, although whether he was seeking reassurance or trying to give it, she wasn't quite sure.

"How many of them are there?" he said, the murmur of his words almost too low to hear.

As the last of the black-coated figures began to climb the steps, Penelope shook her head in reply. She must have seen more than a dozen of these so-called radiant boys emerge from the darkness, but as she turned again to stare at the door, she saw that it was still firmly shut. Had they just walked straight through it? There was only one way to find out if these were men or ghosts.

"Come on," she muttered, squeezing Alfie's hand. "We have to follow them."

The two of them scurried up the steps, Alfie casting a nervous glance back over his shoulder in case any more of these radiant boys emerged from the shadows. As she climbed, Penny's mind ran through the impossibility of what she had just seen. She had thought that the newspaper reports she had read described the movements of a single man, but this army of ghosts gave a much better explanation for the sightings crisscrossing the city.

Reaching the pavement, Penny glanced left and then right, her gaze searching the gloom of the street for any sign of the black-coated figures. Along the grand terrace, most of the houses lay in darkness, their shutters drawn against the evening chill, but beneath the shadow of the Duke of York's statue Penny caught a glimpse of two scurrying figures, their dark coats flapping as they turned to descend the stone steps that led to the Mall.

"This way," she whispered, tugging at Alfie's arm as she followed them in swift pursuit. Reaching the top of the broad stone steps, Penny saw that the shadowy duo were already crossing the Mall, passing beneath the plane trees as they hurried towards the shadows of St James's Park. The rest of the radiant boys seemed to have disappeared into the night, but Penelope was determined that she wouldn't let these last two escape from her sight. She hastened down the steps, cursing the inconvenience of her heels as Alfie hurried to keep up.

Reaching the bottom, Penelope waited for the clattering wheels of a hansom cab to pass before darting across the street. All along the Mall, swathes of bunting festooned with flowers hung from every lamppost, the gaslight throwing into vivid relief the majesty of the decorations. To the south, through the trees, were the towers of Westminster Abbey where King Edward the Seventh would be crowned later that week, whilst looking west lay the stately façade of Buckingham Palace at the bottom of the Mall. But Penny didn't pause to take in these sights, her gaze fixed firmly on the dark figures now slipping inside the park.

"Where are they going now?" Alfie asked breathlessly, peering past Penny as the two of them reached the bounds of St James's Park. The spiked railings almost reached up to Penelope's shoulder as she searched in vain for the gap they must have slipped through. By day, St James's Park was a pleasure garden, filled with trees, shrubberies and ornamental waters, but now it was a wretchedly dark place and Penny tried not to think of the stories her guardian had told her of the thieves and worse who lurked there after nightfall.

"We have to follow them," she said, pointing towards the scurrying shadows of the men as they hurried through the park.

"How?" Alfie replied. "The gates are locked at dusk. I don't even know how they got over the railings so quickly."

Penny glanced over her shoulder, checking that the coast was clear. The Mall was still busy with pedestrians, even at this late hour, but in the shade of the overhanging trees, the two of them could hardly be seen.

"Quick," she said, taking hold of the railings. "You'll have to help me over."

Alfie stared back at her in surprise, taking in her attire with a doubtful glance. With her ankle-length skirt and tailor-made jacket, Penny was hardly dressed to start breaking into one of London's Royal Parks. He was just about to protest when he saw the determined set of her features and realised how useless it would be.

"Here you are," he said with a sigh, slipping his jacket from his shoulders to lay it across the spikes at the top. "If I give you a leg-up, you can be over there in a second. I'll then try to scramble over myself."

"Thank you," Penny replied as Alfie bent down, cradling his hands together so that she could step into them. Taking her weight, Alfie tried not to blush at the sight of Penelope's well-turned ankle, averting his eyes as she clambered up over the railings. With an unladylike groan of effort, Penny dropped down on the other side of the railings, the shrubbery cushioning her fall.

"Are you all right?" Alfie asked.

Penelope got to her feet, brushing stray leaves from her skirt as Alfie scrambled over the railings to join her.

"I'm fine," she replied. She turned to look in the direction of the two men, their shadowy figures already skirting the lake as they hurried westwards. "Come on, we have to find out where they're going."

They followed the figures through the darkness of the park, Alfie wincing at the sound of every twig that crunched underfoot. He glanced down at the gold of his watch chain, trying to banish his fearful imaginings of the thieves who might be lurking in the shadows of the shrubbery. The sudden screech of a waterfowl nesting beneath the dripping trees made him jump in alarm.

Keeping her composure, Penny peered into the gloom. The path the two figures were following was now taking them to the park's westernmost boundary. Beyond the foliage of trees, the ornate gates of Buckingham Palace could be glimpsed, the grand columns of the royal residence rising up behind them. The night was dark, but the windows of the palace shone with a brilliant radiance. From the pinnacle of its flagpole, the Royal Standard fluttered, proclaiming to all that the King was in residence tonight.

Desperate not to lose the two figures as they flitted between the trees, Penelope picked her way through the undergrowth, Alfie following close behind. The men were less than twenty feet away now, the glow of the street lamps beyond the park illuminating the glowing-green tint of their skin, which could just be glimpsed between the dark folds of their scarves. As Penny stepped beneath the shade of a scarlet oak, the warning honk of a goose nesting in the undergrowth caused the two men to glance back in their direction.

Penelope froze. Behind her, she heard Alfie's muttered curse as the first of the black-coated figures took a step towards the source of the sound. For a second his scarf slipped, causing

Penny to silently gasp in surprise. The newspapers had described these mysterious figures as radiant boys, but until this very moment she hadn't truly realised why.

The face staring back at them was the face of a boy not much older than Alfie himself. The boy's features were drawn in a haunted frown, but his skin glowed iridescently as if lit from within. From the darkness of the trees, Penelope prayed that he couldn't see them.

The sound of the second man's voice turned the boy's gaze back to the palace. Penelope couldn't make out the words, but the meaning was clear. Pulling the scarf back over his face, the boy followed his companion as they slipped through the park railings without a pause, their shadows scurrying towards the palace.

"That was close," Alfie muttered in relief. "But surely they can't be heading for the palace gates."

Shaking her head, Penny hurried to the railings. There was no time now to try and climb over. All she could do was watch as the black-coated figures closed in on the grand edifice. Outside the palace gates, a soldier stood guard outside his sentry box, his scarlet tunic and black bearskin cap illuminated by the light falling from a nearby lamppost. His gaze was fixed straight ahead, unaware of the two shadowy figures now slipping like ghosts through the high, spiked gates.

Alfie appeared at her shoulder, peering through

the park railings to see the figures disappear into the shadows of the palace.

"What are they doing?"

Penelope shook her head again. She had no idea. Was this yet another daring theft to add to the haul of the Crown Jewels? Thinking quickly, she glanced again at the guard standing sentry at the gates. If she tried to raise the alarm now, she knew that she wouldn't be believed. There was no way the soldier would think that thieves could have walked through the gates of the palace without his having seen them. He was more likely to call the police and have her and Alfie arrested for trespassing in the Royal Park. There was only one person who might possibly believe that they had watched the shadowy figures walk through solid iron.

"We have to tell Inspector Drake what we've seen tonight," she said, staring into the darkness where the radiant boys had disappeared. There was no sign now of any movement in the shadows, but the palace windows still shone brightly. If by any miracle they had found their way inside, then they would soon be discovered. "Surely this will clear Monty's name."

X

Drake leaned across the table, fixing Monty with an intimidating stare.

"I am losing my patience, Mr Flinch. It has been a long night and your lack of cooperation is proving to be an irritation." He glanced at the burly figure of the police constable hovering over his shoulder in the cramped interrogation room. "I hope it won't be necessary for me to ask Constable Taylor here to loosen your tongue."

Monty shrank back in his chair. The actor's face was drawn, dark circles inked beneath his eyes whilst his features bristled with the beginnings of a beard. Next to him, Mr Wigram blinked hard and then frowned.

"And I do hope you are not threatening my client, Inspector Drake. It is enough of a scandal that you have held him here for so long without a single shred of evidence."

Drake eyed the figure of the elderly lawyer with disdain.

"The gravity of the situation demands that I take every appropriate action to find out the truth. May I remind you that the charge of treason is a capital crime. As for evidence, I have Montgomery Flinch's own confession printed in the pages of *The Penny Dreadful*, whereas your client has been unable to even provide me with an alibi for the night of the tenth of May."

"I told you," Monty protested, his eyes wild with a look of injured innocence. "I spent the evening at a tavern in Soho."

Drake sneered at his reply.

"But you appear to have indulged too heavily to remember exactly which one. My men have visited every public house in the area, but not one of the landlords and barmaids we have questioned recollect seeing Montgomery Flinch on the night in question."

Beside Monty, Wigram let out an exasperated sigh. His prediction that Monty's drinking would end in *The Penny Dreadful*'s ruin seemed to be coming true in a most unexpected fashion.

"And that's not all," Drake continued. "As a matter of fact, our investigations are finding the identity of Montgomery Flinch to be as much of a mystery as his whereabouts on the night of the tenth of May. No birth certificate, no mention of his name in parish records or census returns – in fact, the first time the name of Montgomery Flinch appears in print is in the pages of *The*

Penny Dreadful in 1899. A mere three years ago."

As Monty shrank further into his seat, Wigram began to stutter out an explanation, the lawyer's own face now pale.

"Records can be lost," he began. "Last winter, at the offices of *The Penny Dreadful*, we had the misfortune of losing many of Mr Flinch's personal documents when our printer's assistant mistook them for kindling for the fire."

"A likely story," Drake snapped in reply. "Until I hear a cast-iron alibi and see proof of Montgomery Flinch's identity, then I am keeping your client here, Mr Wigram, on the authority of the Crown no less. Must I remind you that these are dangerous times – there are whispers of war from overseas and rumours of foreign agents on the prowl. For all I know, Montgomery Flinch might be a spy whose plot is to disrupt the coronation itself."

He turned his accusatory stare back towards Monty, the dishevelled actor blanching under its glare.

"*Wosind die Kronjuwelen, Herr Flinch?*"

Monty stared back blankly at the detective before bursting into tears.

"I don't know what you mean!" he wailed. "Why do you insist on torturing me like this?"

Inspector Drake held his gaze, his face intent as he inspected Monty's anguished expression.

"Oh, you're good, Mr Flinch," he said finally. "I have to give you that. Keeping up this pretence of cowardice and ignorance even though all of London knows that your intricate tales of terror make lesser minds quail."

Before Drake could press Monty further, there came a rap on the door of the interrogation room. The face of a police constable peered around the frame.

"I'm sorry to interrupt, sir, but I've got a visitor for Mr Flinch at the front desk. It's a young lady who says that she's his niece: one Miss Penelope Tredwell."

At this announcement, a flicker of irritation flashed across the detective's face, but then Inspector Drake rearranged his features into a thin smile.

"You had better take him back to his cell then, Constable Richards. I am sure Mr Flinch and his niece will have plenty to discuss." He turned towards Monty again, his dark eyes narrowing as he spoke. "Perhaps she can convince you to reveal the truth behind your treasonous scheme. It might be the last chance you have."

"You have to get me out of this accursed place, Penelope," Monty wailed. "I cannot survive for another second here. I have been fingerprinted, threatened, poked and prodded to the brink of my tolerance. The scant meals that I have been served are not even fit for a dog, and I haven't had a drink for days. They won't even allow me a razor to shave with."

Beneath the barred window of his cell, Monty sat on the edge of a rough wooden bench. A grubby blanket was draped across his lap and he stared up at Penny with a woebegone look.

"You have to tell Inspector Drake the truth," he pleaded, reaching out towards her with a trembling hand. "It is the only chance we have of convincing him that I didn't steal the Crown Jewels. The man is deluded – he's even claiming that Montgomery Flinch could be a foreign spy."

The rattle of a truncheon against the bars of the cell caused Monty to jump in fright. Stationed by the cell door, the watching police constable fixed him with a warning glare, brandishing his nightstick with a swagger.

"Remember what I told you, Flinch," he rasped. "No funny business, else you'll be feeling the edge of my temper again."

Monty shrank back on the bench, drawing the blanket up around him defensively.

With an impatient sniff, the police constable nodded his satisfaction.

"One more minute – that's all the both of you are getting with him."

Penelope glanced across at her guardian. Standing facing Monty, the elderly lawyer's features looked almost as worn as the actor's, a testimony to the long night he had spent sitting by his side as they fielded Inspector Drake's endless questions.

"Perhaps Monty is right," Wigram said softly. "I seem unable to persuade the police of Montgomery Flinch's innocence in regard to these ridiculous charges. And the questions that Inspector Drake has started to ask about Flinch's real identity are rather too close to the bone. It might be the time to reveal the true origin of his tale of *The Thief Who Wasn't There*."

Penelope shook her head. The sunlight slanting through the window of the cell revealed the shadows beneath her own eyes, but there was a gleam of illumination in her gaze.

"I have seen him," she replied simply. "*The Thief Who Wasn't There* isn't fiction – the Black Crow is real. And as soon as I tell Inspector Drake what I witnessed last night, he will have no choice but to let you go, Monty. You just need to stay strong for a little while longer."

As Monty flushed, fresh hope shining in his eyes, the constable swung open the cell door with a clang.

"Time's up," he barked.

Pulling her gloves on, Penny gave Monty a reassuring nod.

"I will see you again soon."

As Wigram escorted her out of the cell, the police constable locked the door again, triple-bolting it as Monty stared back at them through the bars. Turning to lead them out of the cells, the policeman glanced down at Penelope in surprise as she stood barring his path.

"I would like to see Inspector Drake," Penny informed him. "I have information about the theft of the Crown Jewels – information that exonerates my uncle."

The walls of the inspector's office were tapestried with police notices: photographs of suspects, wanted posters and crime-scene sketches. A height-gauge leaned against the furthest wall, whilst arranged on the shelves above this were records, registers and photographic albums – the modern detective's tools of identification.

With Wigram by her side, Penelope stood in front of Inspector Drake's desk, the detective staring at them both with a look of weary disdain. He drummed his fingers on the lid of a snuff box sitting on his desk, the pile of papers next to it threatening to topple with every vibration. With a sigh, Drake glanced down at the notebook where he had recorded Penelope's statement, the lines of text trailing away as his growing sense of disbelief won the day.

"I do not quite know what to say, Miss Tredwell," he began. "You expect me to believe that instead of Montgomery Flinch being behind this treasonous crime, it was instead instigated by a troop of black-coated thieves whose skin glows green? A legion of ghostly figures who stalk the streets of the city at night and who you claim to have seen walk through the walls of Buckingham Palace last night?"

Penelope felt a blush reddening her cheeks as Inspector Drake recounted to her exactly what she had said. Suddenly she realised how ridiculous the whole thing sounded.

"And what's more," Drake continued, "you report that these unlikely thieves do not dwell in the expected places where unquiet spirits are known to cluster: cemeteries, graveyards and suchlike, but are instead resident at the distinguished Society for the Advancement of Science. A society that is located on one of the most exclusive streets in the city – Carlton House Terrace – allowing these light-fingered spectres to count earls and ambassadors, dukes and countesses amongst their neighbours."

Penny tried to interrupt, but the inspector held up a warning hand as he looked up from his notebook.

"Your loyalty to your uncle is admirable, Miss Tredwell, and I can see that you have inherited his talent for inventing such astounding stories, although I have heard that Montgomery Flinch's tales are said to have a modicum more believability than this preposterous tale you have spun me."

"It's not a story," Penny replied, her complexion almost scarlet now.

Inspector Drake waved her words away with a dismissive flick of his wrist. He turned his gaze instead to Mr Wigram, the lawyer resting his hands protectively on his young charge's shoulders.

"And are you behind this charade too?" the detective spat, finding a suitable target at last for his anger. "The desperation of your client is plain to see if he thinks such ludicrous inventions can clear his name." He turned his glare back towards Penelope. "And if you weren't a mere child, I'd have a mind to charge you with conspiracy to boot."

"But the palace," Penelope protested. "If you would just investigate what I saw last night—"

"I am investigating the theft of the Crown Jewels," Drake replied with a barely concealed contempt in his words. "Do you not think I would have heard if the grounds of Buckingham Palace had been breached by intruders?" His face twisted in fury as he jabbed his finger towards the door. "Now, get out before I have you both arrested as well!"

Penelope felt the weight of her guardian's hand on her shoulder as he steered her to the door. As it closed behind them, they heard a sudden fluttering sound as Drake flung his notebook against the wall with a curse. Greeting them with a mocking grin, the waiting police constable escorted them down the long corridor that led past the cells, the anguished shouts of the prisoners there reminding Penny of Monty's plight.

Her cheeks burned as Inspector Drake's words rang in her ears. *If you weren't a mere child, I'd have a mind to charge you...* How could she possibly convince his closed mind that she was telling the truth? No matter what she said now, there was no way the detective would believe her.

As the police constable ushered them unceremoniously through the front doors of New Scotland Yard, Wigram and Penelope emerged blinking into the sunshine. The Thames lay directly in front of them and, from the Palace of Westminster on their right, Penelope could hear the chimes of Big Ben telling her how much of the morning she had already wasted. As they walked along the Embankment, Wigram turned towards her, his expression grave.

"There are dark forces at work here, Penny. The police dismiss all my legal arguments and won't even countenance the prospect of releasing Mr Maples on bail. If I am to procure his release, I must consult now with a fellow from Gray's Inn: one of the finest criminal barristers in the land. I am sure he will see a way to get these ridiculous charges dismissed."

He flagged down a passing hansom cab,

instructing the driver to take him to no. 8 South Square. As he climbed up into the carriage, Wigram turned back to Penelope, still standing on the pavement.

"You must return home, Penny," he told her. "I do not wish you to place yourself in any further danger after your misadventures of last night."

With a reluctant nod, Penny agreed to her guardian's request and, thus satisfied, Wigram settled back into his seat, instructing the driver to depart with a rap on the roof of the cab. With a tug of the reins, the cab driver set off down the Embankment, and Penelope slowly uncrossed her fingers as she watched the vehicle join the stream of traffic heading along the bank of the Thames.

Straightening her jacket, she turned right, heading down Derby Gate towards St James's Park. Carlton House Terrace and the Society for the Advancement of Science was less than a quarter of an hour's walk away. Penny's eyes seemed to flash fire as the sunlight caught them, and a look of determination framed her softly chiselled chin. If the police wouldn't investigate what she had seen, then it would be down to her to solve this mystery.

XI

The stucco-white façade of Carlton House Terrace shone with an opulent splendour in the late morning sunshine, the grand houses looking even more imposing than they had yesterday evening. Dressed in a serge-blue suit, her jacket and skirt cut in the latest continental style, Penelope climbed the steps to No. 8 Carlton House Terrace, the shade of the porch sheltering her from the full glare of the sun.

With her hair swept high atop her head, Penny looked much older than her fifteen years. The admiring glances she had drawn from passing gentlemen on her journey here had been a telling rebuke to Inspector Drake's dismissal of her as a mere child. She glanced down at the nameplate fixed beside the door: *The Society for the Advancement of Science*. It was time to find out what discoveries she could make here.

She pressed the bell push, an answering ring sounding from within. Penelope waited, her patience stretching as the seconds passed. She pressed the doorbell again, then, when no answer was forthcoming, she reached down to try the handle. With a gentle push, the door opened and, glancing back over her shoulder, Penny stepped inside.

She stifled a gasp as she took in her surroundings. The grandeur of the entrance hall was beyond even the expectations that had been raised by the building's exterior. A three-flight black marble staircase swept up in front of Penelope, flanked by two grand torchères, whilst ornate chandeliers hung from the cream-and-gold corniced ceiling. The portraits of distinguished scientists filled the walls: Isaac Newton, Johannes Kepler, William Hershel and Charles Darwin, their erudite gazes eyeing her with interest. Penny stepped forward in awe, her heels clicking across the black-and-white tiled floor.

The sound of a cough stopped her in her tracks. Penelope turned to see the figure of an elderly man with a prodigious beard, his shock of white hair tipping forward as he peered at her over his spectacles, the lenses thicker than bottle tops.

"Ah bonjour, madame," he exclaimed, seizing hold of Penelope's hand in a dusty handshake. "The conference has already started, but Professor Röntgen will be delighted to discover that you have arrived here at last."

Speechless with surprise, Penelope felt the

elderly scientist take hold of her arm.

"It's this way, madame," he said, gesturing past the staircase towards a long corridor. "Let me escort you to the lecture room before I return to my own studies."

Without a chance to protest, Penelope was hurried along the corridor, passing on her left a bronzed bust of Copernicus. A sense of unease crept into her mind. It was almost as if she was expected. A tiny frisson of fear slithered down her spine as she remembered the sight of the black-clad figures taking flight from the basement of the Society last night. Surely she hadn't been spotted?

Unaware of her concern, Penelope's escort led her along the white-panelled corridor. Through the open doors they passed, Penny caught glimpses of laboratories filled with scientific equipment: monocular microscopes, vacuum pumps, spectroscopes and electrostatic generators. Noting her interest, the white-bearded scientist paused at one of the open doors.

"You must forgive me, madame. I forgot to introduce myself. I am Dr John Hughlings Jackson and this is my domain." He gestured inside the laboratory to where a half-dissected cadaver was laid out on a table, the stench of formaldehyde creeping out into the corridor. With an inquisitive eye, Penny saw that the skin on the corpse's head was peeled back, the top of the skull sawn away to reveal the brain beneath. "The realm of flesh and blood is where my interest lies, not that invisible world that you and Professor Röntgen meddle in. What a magnificent creature man is," Dr Jackson exclaimed, his little eyes blinking behind his spectacles. "And there is still so much for us to discover. Do you know that we have begun to create a map of the human brain?"

Penelope shook her head, trying to disguise her confusion. What could be the connection here with the mystery of the radiant boys? She listened intently as Dr Jackson explained his theory of how electrical discharges from the brain controlled a person's movements.

"Ach, listen to me," he said finally, pushing his spectacles back up his nose. "Here I am, boring you with my endeavours, when you have your own work to attend to." The elderly scientist took hold of Penelope's arm again, hurrying her through a set of double doors to a broad gallery. Ahead of them, a second set of double doors were closed and the muffled sound of a man's voice could just be heard through them. "The conference is being held in the Cavendish Suite," Dr Jackson said, stepping forward to silently open the left-hand door. Peering inside, he lowered his voice as he gestured for Penelope to enter. "Professor Röntgen is still making his opening remarks, madame. When he heard that your train from Dover had been delayed, he was concerned that you would miss his opening address but do not fear, a place has been set for you at the table."

Through the open door, Penelope could see a long dark walnut table, a dozen chairs set on either side. The faces of their occupants were all turned towards the figure holding forth at the head of the table. There stood a tall, loose-limbed man dressed in a dark-blue sack suit, his hands gesticulating like an animated gust of wind. He must have been approaching his sixtieth year, but his black hair stood straight up from his forehead as if electrified by his own enthusiasm, whilst his beard was even more prodigious than Dr Jackson's, although its hue was of a somewhat darker shade. This was Professor Röntgen. As the Wedgwood-blue carpet swallowed the sound of her heels, Penny slipped into the empty seat at the table, Dr Jackson softly closing the door behind her.

"So I would like to thank you, gentlemen, for attending this inaugural conference of the Society for the Advancement of Science." Professor Röntgen's deep voice was marked with a Germanic accent. "Around this table here today we have some of the finest minds in physics – from Great Britain, France, New Zealand and my own native Germany to name but a few."

Unnoticed by the others, Penelope's heart

began to race. She wasn't meant to be here, that much was clear. On the table in front of her a place card had been set and, reaching forward, she turned this towards her so that she could read the name.

Mme Marie Curie

The name snagged in Penelope's mind, somehow familiar to her from the scientific journals that she read when searching for inspiration for Montgomery Flinch's latest tale. She recalled an article she had read about the researches of this remarkable scientist, Polish-born but now living in France with her husband, Pierre, and how they had discovered a strange new phenomenon called radioactivity. At the time, Penelope had been heartened to see a woman making her mark in the scientific community, taking inspiration for her own ambition, but now she realised that she could be its beneficiary as well. This was who Dr Jackson had mistaken her for – Madame Marie Curie.

Penny glanced up at the gentlemen arranged around the table, all moustaches, beards and spectacles. Could she dare to hope that they would all make the same mistake?

"I have a proposal for you all," Professor Röntgen continued, his penetrating gaze darting round the table. "That we should set aside all thoughts of national interest, and instead work together for the advancement of science."

He reached down towards the apparatus set out at the head of the table: the glass bulb of a vacuum tube mounted on a stand, and two copper wires connecting this to a large induction coil. With a flick of a switch, the device crackled into life, blue sparks shimmering across the tightly wound copper coils as the vacuum tube began to glow with a yellow-green light. Penelope watched spellbound, the eerie glow instantly reminding her of the luminescent features of the radiant boys who she had seen leaving this very place last night. Professor Röntgen passed his hand between the vacuum tube and the buzzing electrical coil, the yellowish-green light playing across the surface of his skin.

"Six years ago, when I discovered the existence of X-rays," he said, "I did not realise the remarkable advances that this extraordinary phenomena would bring. These invisible rays with the power to peel back the layers of reality; stripping flesh from bone to reveal shadow pictures of what lies beneath our very skin. How they could penetrate most forms of solid matter, seemingly without harm, the thickness of the material no bar to their great power." His gleaming eyes reflected the iridescent glow of the vacuum tube, slowly fading to grey as he switched the electrical current off. "Since then the further discoveries we have all made have thrown a new light on this invisible world: electromagnetic radiation, the identification of the electron, and discovering the particles of which atoms are made. The last century was an age of steam, but working together at the dawn of this new century, we can lead the way into a new atomic age."

Professor Röntgen's audience greeted his remarks with an appreciative murmur.

"There are more discoveries to be made," he told them, his eyes still shining with a missionary zeal. "I am certain of this. These rays are a phenomenon of the ether, and perhaps soon we will be able to harness their power to transcend the physical laws that bind us."

From Penelope's side of the table, a man with a drooping moustache and receding hairline raised his voice in protest.

"Surely the laws of nature are fixed?" he scoffed. "These invisible rays of yours are all very well, Röntgen, but even they have to obey the fundamental rules of the universe."

Professor Röntgen stared back at the man, a mischievous smile playing around his lips.

"Perhaps, Professor Rutherford, perhaps, but don't your own experiments suggest that even the atom can be broken through the application of radiation? I read your paper on *The Theory of Atomic Disintegration* with interest, but a few years ago this suggestion would have been seen as heresy by most scientists."

As Professor Rutherford blustered in reply, Röntgen's gaze fell on Penelope. He paused for a moment, his smile broadening as he took in the presence of her feminine charms.

"I am delighted to say, gentlemen, that another distinguished mind has joined us here today," he announced. "Unfortunately her husband could not make the journey from France, but Madame Curie should be able to share with us some of the momentous discoveries that they have made."

XII

Around the table every gaze turned towards Penelope, the men's eyebrows raised at the sight of the exotic bloom of her serge-blue suit amidst their sea of grey. With a nervous smile, she greeted their attention, silently praying she could get away with this masquerade.

"I must say, Madame Curie," Röntgen continued, a puzzled frown slowly spreading across his forehead as he peered more closely at Penelope. "The smudged portrait that accompanied your paper in the recent *Quarterly Journal of Microscopical Science* did not do justice to your charms."

A murmur of agreement rippled around the table, the scientists gathered there more accustomed to the company of test tubes and electrometers than a young woman of some considerable beauty.

"And may I ask you, madame, what you think of this challenge I have set? Do you agree that with the application of science we will be able to find a way to overcome the limits of the physical realm?"

Penelope blinked, her heart racing beneath her jacket as the room awaited her reply. With a timorous cough, she tried to compose herself.

"It is an admirable aim," she replied, disguising her English accent with a tremulous continental quaver. "But one thing that you said intrigued me, Professor Röntgen, and I wondered if I could press you on it."

"Of course," Röntgen replied magnanimously. "That is the purpose of this conference – to bring new insights to the discoveries we have made."

Penelope tried to shape the myriad questions spiralling around her mind. She couldn't shake the image of the curious yellow-green glow that had clung to the vacuum tube; this strange luminescence emanating from the faces of the radiant boys.

"When you say that we might one day control the powers of these invisible rays, what exactly do you think might be possible? Could we perhaps harness their penetrative power to enable a man to walk through walls?"

A ripple of amusement greeted her remarks, the assembled scientists sniggering into their moustaches at the ridiculous nature of the question. But Professor Röntgen stood there stony-faced, his expression frozen as a look of alarm flashed in his eyes. Then, suddenly realising that every gaze in the room had turned back to him to await his reply, the professor regained his composure.

"Anything is possible, madame," he said, his quick and penetrating eyes peering more closely at Penelope. "Your own remarkable discoveries have surely shown you this. But such a feat, for the moment, lies beyond our grasp. A parlour trick for the stage magician, perhaps, rather than the pursuit of any serious scientist."

"Hear! Hear!" The others murmured their approval, relieved to see this impertinent woman put in her place.

The chime of a gong echoed outside the lecture room and, glancing at his watch, Röntgen gestured towards the doors behind him.

"Lunch will be served in the dining room, gentlemen," he announced as these double doors swung open to reveal a second large room. This space was filled with another long table, almost a mirror of the first, but this time covered with a great expanse of tablecloth upon which was set a veritable feast. Professor Röntgen paused to correct himself. "Gentlemen and lady, I should say. We shall have the opportunity to recommence our discussion after our repast."

The scientists eagerly rose from their chairs, the fragrance of roast beef and the steam of soup beckoning them towards the dining room.

Professor Röntgen, though, remained where he was standing, watching Penelope with a hard-eyed stare. From the glower on his face, Penny could tell that her question had been an unwelcome one. As she followed the rest of the bewhiskered scientists out of the lecture room, the professor was waiting for her by the door.

"I am delighted that you could join us here today, Madame Curie," he began, his manner superficially solicitous as he peered intently at Penelope, taking in her unlined countenance and the youthful style of her attire. "And I must admit I was rather intrigued by your question just now. The mysteries of the atomic world are yet to be fully revealed, but the power that we could harness might well be beyond compare. Perhaps over lunch we could discuss your own experiments and the discoveries that you have made. It may be the case that we are working at a common purpose."

Penelope could see a gleam of suspicion in the scientist's eyes, the hardness of his gaze belying the warmth of his words.

"Of course, I would be delighted to," she replied, her continental accent faltering as she frantically tried to think of a way to escape such a fate. She couldn't keep up this façade for much longer. Penelope's command of French was rudimentary at best whilst her Polish was non-existent – if Professor Röntgen began to quiz her about her scientific experimentation she would be discovered at once. Besides, if the train from Dover had only been delayed, then Madame Curie herself might arrive at any moment. In desperation, Penny resorted to euphemism. "But first I must attend to my *toilette*. Could you pray tell me where I could wash my hands before lunch?"

Professor Röntgen blushed, Penelope's question momentarily throwing him off his guard.

"Of course, of course," he harrumphed, tugging at his beard with a flustered gesture. "The *waschraum* is just along the corridor on the right." He gestured towards a narrow passageway that lay between the two rooms, branching off to the left and to the right. "I will save you a seat next to me at the dining table and I look forward to continuing our discussion then."

With a nod of gratitude, Penny turned right down the corridor, her heels clicking on the polished tiles. As she walked, she could feel Röntgen's eyes on her back, his suspicious gaze trying to penetrate her disguise like one of his X-rays.

Reaching the door he had indicated, Penelope pushed it open and stepped inside. Beneath a miniature chandelier, a marble sink was set in front of a mirror and along from this, behind a half-open door, she could glimpse the water closet. Penny rested her hands on the marble, staring into the mirror to gather her thoughts.

Professor Röntgen knew something of these radiant boys, she was sure of it. The strange green glow that had played across his skin as he passed his hand across the scientific apparatus had been an eerie reflection of their complexion. He had spoken of how his discovery had peeled back the layers of reality – of invisible rays that could pass through solid matter without the slightest of harm, and how one day he would harness their power to bend the very laws of nature to his will. And when she had asked if he thought this might allow a living man to walk through walls, Röntgen's agitated reaction told her that she was on the trail of the truth.

Her mind returned to the anonymous letter with its illustration of a black crow. Its author had mentioned experiments. Had Professor Röntgen conducted these? If she could find his laboratory, then perhaps she would find the answers she was searching for.

From the corridor outside, she heard a commotion: the shrill tone of a woman's voice raised in protest, the accent distinctly continental. Peering around the edge of the washroom door, Penelope saw Professor Röntgen in agitated conversation with Dr Jackson, the elderly scientist who had first escorted her to the lecture room. Standing in front of the two men was a woman dressed in a high-collared black dress and coat, her stern features arranged into an expression of outrage.

"I have never been so insulted in my life!" the woman exclaimed with a stamp of her foot. "How dare you say that I am not Madame Marie Curie!"

The scientist's gestures were animated, the frown lining Röntgen's brow deepening as he listened to her protests. Penny couldn't catch every word but the message was clear. The arrival of the real Madame Curie had put an untimely end to her deception.

Slipping out of the cloakroom, Penelope trod lightly as she tiptoed down the corridor, almost holding her breath until she turned the corner. Thinking fast, she tried to work out her next move. A gentlemanly sense of decorum might give her a few minutes until Röntgen and Jackson discovered her disappearance from the lavatory. From the white-panelled walls, portraits of famous scientists watched her as she crept forward, their inquisitive stares reflecting her own as she peered into the mysterious rooms that lined the corridor. She could see storage cabinets filled with scientific equipment, blackboards covered in equations, jars of chemicals and Tesla coils, even cadavers preserved in various states of dissection, but nothing that seemed to reveal the secrets of the radiant boys.

At the end of the corridor stood a stairwell and

Penelope's gaze followed this down. Last night she had watched a flock of ghostly figures emerge from the depths of this building. This was her chance to find out exactly where they had come from.

As she hurried down the narrow flight of stairs, Penny's mind ran over what she had seen. The figures she had watched step out from the tradesmen's entrance had been living men, she was sure of this. She recalled the fear that haunted the gaze of the boy she had followed through St James's Park, the scarf falling from his features to reveal a glowing green countenance. What manner of experiment could create such a face?

Reaching the bottom of the stairwell, Penelope stared into the gloom. She could see a wide hall, seemingly running the length of the building, with blackboards fixed to the walls. Penny glanced at the nearest of these, trying to decipher the chalked symbols, numbers and equations, far beyond her own understanding. How could she even tell if this held the answers she was searching for? The sound of raised voices from the floor above caused Penny to glance upwards in alarm.

"But if this is the real Madame Curie, then who on earth was that other woman?" She instantly recognised Professor Röntgen's clipped tones. "Our work here is of the utmost importance for the future of mankind; we cannot just let any passing waifs and strays wander in from the street."

In reply, the stuttering sound of Dr Jackson's voice echoed down the stairwell.

"I am sorry, my dear professor. I had not before seen a portrait of Madame Curie, and when the first young woman arrived at the very time when the delegates were expected, I could not imagine who else it would be."

At the sound of their footsteps descending the stairs Penelope sprang into action. She hurried forward, wincing at every sound that her footsteps made on the patterned tiles. She tried the first door on her right, but then groaned in frustration as she found it was locked. It was the same with the next one and the next again, the solid oak doors denying her a hiding place. From the stairwell, Professor Röntgen's grumbling reply grew louder still. In another moment she would be discovered.

Turning in desperation, Penny spotted a grubby-looking door with a sign reading "STOREROOM". Lunging for the handle, the door opened at a push and she quickly slipped inside, closing the door behind her. Breathing heavily she stood there in the gloom, listening as Röntgen and Jackson reached the bottom of the stairs.

"I want every room down here secured," the professor snapped, his shoes squeaking across the tiled floor. "My experimental equipment is of incalculable value; I cannot risk it falling into the hands of some sneak thief."

"I hardly think the young lady looked like a thief," Dr Jackson replied in a mollifying tone.

"Appearances can be deceptive. Surely you have learned that by now."

An answering jangle of keys gave Professor Röntgen the reply he was looking for.

With her back pressed against the door, Penny glanced round her surroundings for the first time. Rather than a storeroom filled with scientific equipment, she found herself standing in a narrow passageway, its surface gently sloping upwards into the darkness. The only source of light was that seeping through the doorframe, the keyhole illuminating a scratched picture etched into the wood-panelled wall. Penelope gasped. It was the outline of a bird – a black crow, in fact – poised as if it was about to take flight.

She cringed as the sound of footsteps drew near. She couldn't let herself be discovered here, not now she had found this first clue. Penny reached out with her hand, feeling the scratches beneath her fingers: the curve of the crow's beak and the ruffled plumage of its feathers. The real Black Crow, whose anonymous letter had inspired the story of *The Thief Who Wasn't There*, must have stood in this very spot. Keeping her hand against the wood-panelled wall, Penelope crept forward into the darkness. She had to find out where this passageway led.

From behind her, she heard the rattle of the door handle. Penny froze, waiting for the moment of discovery. Then, with a scraping sound, she heard the turn of a key in the lock, followed by muffled footsteps walking away. She let out a silent sigh of relief. For the moment, she was safe.

Penelope shuffled forward, picking her steps carefully in the darkness. The air around her was cool and crisp and goose pimples pricked at her skin. Penny shivered, thoughts of the black-coated figures she had seen last night crowding her thoughts. She peered into the gloom. She could only hope that she would not meet them here unawares.

Ahead of her, the passage seemed to be coming to an end and the faint outline of a door was just visible in the darkness. Penny stumbled slightly as she hurried towards this, praying that this way out hadn't been similarly locked. As she reached for the handle, she stood there for a moment, her ear pressed to the door to try to ascertain what was on the other side. There was only silence.

Opening the door carefully, Penelope peered through the gap. She could see silent rows of figures hanging in the darkness, and for a second she drew back in fear. Then, as her eyes adjusted to the gloom, a relieved smile crept over her lips as Penny realised her mistake. The dark shapes she could see were not people, but uniforms draped over clothes hangers. She stepped forward, brushing her way past the first row of coats to see another door directly ahead.

Penelope's smile broadened to a grin. This was a plot twist that even Montgomery Flinch would dismiss as far-fetched: a secret passage that led to what looked like a wardrobe. Reaching out, she cautiously pushed at this second door, the wardrobe slowly opening to reveal an empty room.

With a prudent glance around her, Penny stepped out into the well-lit room. A large window overlooked the Duke of York's statue and steps, and on the white-panelled walls several paintings were hung: military scenes showing cavalry charges, naval engagements and distinguished portraits of high-ranking officers, the style of their uniforms strangely unfamiliar.

Penny glanced back into the wardrobe to inspect the clothes that were hanging there. In the first row, she could see more than a dozen dark-blue jackets, their brass buttons emblazoned with crowns and anchors revealing which branch of the military they belonged to, but it was the garments hanging on the second row that caused Penelope to catch her breath. At first glance, they were almost nondescript: bulky black greatcoats, their collars swathed with long, dark scarves. It was when she had seen them last that made her pulse race with fear. These were the clothes worn by the radiant boys.

Reaching into the wardrobe again, she checked through the pockets of the greatcoats, frantically searching for clues. All of these seemed empty, but buried deep in the inside pocket of the second last, she found what looked like a screwed-up magazine. Opening this out, her eyes sparkled with triumph as she saw the front cover of *The Penny Dreadful*, its cover line proclaiming the return of Montgomery Flinch with his tale of *The Thief Who Wasn't There*. She knew now that she was on the right trail.

Pocketing the magazine, Penelope carefully closed the wardrobe door, her eyes darting around the room to search for further clues. If this was where the radiant boys disguised themselves, then Professor Röntgen's laboratory had to be close by. Facing the window, a single door led out of the room. She walked towards this, a renewed sense of purpose in her step.

Penny opened the door to reveal a reception hall even grander than the one that had greeted her on her entrance to the Society. Its panelled walls were hung with gilt-framed portraits, whilst a grand marble staircase spiralled up towards a vaulted ceiling, gold and crystal chandeliers suspended from it like a constellation of stars.

Puzzled, Penelope wandered through the hall, gazing upwards as she tried to work out exactly where she was.

"*Kannich ihnen helfen, madame?*"

Penelope turned at the sound of the voice, a moustachioed man in a smart tweed suit stepping out to greet her from an adjoining room. She stared back at him nonplussed, her mind scrabbling to translate his words.

"Can I help you, madam?" the man repeated, his English impeccable.

Penelope frowned in confusion.

"I don't know," she replied truthfully, slowly shaking her head. "I'm not quite sure where I am."

A frown creased the man's forehead, mirroring Penelope's own. He gestured impatiently at the largest portrait hanging on the wall between them. There, the figure of a man dressed in a military uniform gazed down at them both with an arrogant stare. Penelope recognised him at once, his image instantly familiar from the newspaper pages: Kaiser Wilhelm the Second, King of Prussia and Emperor of Germany.

"This is the Imperial German Embassy," the man replied brusquely. "What exactly is your business here?"

XIII

"And what did you say then?" Alfie asked eagerly, resting his chin on his hands as he waited for Penelope to continue her story.

Behind her desk at *The Penny Dreadful*, Penny brushed a stray lock of her hair from her eyes; the hair piled high upon her head was slowly descending under the heat of the day.

"I told him I had been waiting for my uncle by the statue of the Duke of York, but that I had suddenly felt somewhat overcome by the sun. How I had wandered into the embassy in search of a place to recover myself. After he fetched me a reviving glass of water, I bid him good day and then made a hasty exit."

Alfie let out a low whistle, unable to hide his amazement at the story she had told him.

"And you did all of this yesterday, while I was stuck at the printers pulping the July edition. The next time you go impersonating a distinguished scientist you'll have to let me come along too." Alfie screwed up his features to create a threatening countenance. "I quite fancy the chance of playing the part of Dr Jekyll."

Penelope smiled. "I think you are confusing Dr Jekyll with the character of Mr Hyde. Besides, these are purely fictional creations, unlike our Black Crow, it seems." Reaching into her pocket she drew out the creased edition of the magazine she had found hidden in the greatcoat pocket. "It even appears that one of the radiant boys is an avid reader of *The Penny Dreadful*."

Alfie scratched his head, his expression of affected menace quickly fading to be replaced by a look of pure puzzlement.

"I still don't understand how you ended up in the Imperial German Embassy. Why take the trouble of hiding a secret passage inside a wardrobe when the two houses are just next door to each other?"

Penny narrowed her eyes at Alfie speaking out loud the very same question that she had asked herself.

"Because this is something that they wish to hide," she replied. "The secret of the radiant boys. There is a connection between the embassy and the Society for the Advancement of Science, and I am sure Professor Röntgen is at the heart of it. He is of German extraction, after all."

Alfie scowled. The newspapers were filled every day with stories of German duplicity; how by strengthening his navy the Kaiser would soon threaten the might of the British Empire itself. The printer's assistant had read *The Battle of Dorking* and other tales of invasion, these stories describing in lurid prose how the very shores of England would soon be overrun by German soldiers.

"This is a dangerous business," he said, his words echoing Penny's guardian's own. "We need to alert the authorities."

Penny slowly shook her head, trying to marshal the facts she had uncovered in her mind.

"I've already tried that," she replied bitterly. "Inspector Drake just accused me of wasting his time. He thinks that I invented the story about the figures we saw sneaking into the palace in order to get Monty off the hook. He won't believe a word that I say."

"Well, we need to tell Mr Wigram at least. This is too large a mystery for you to solve alone."

Penelope frowned. Her guardian had not long returned from New Scotland Yard, his latest efforts to win Monty's release for the moment unsuccessful. With the strain of the long nights and even longer days showing on his features, Wigram had quickly left for the printers in order to negotiate a further delay to their overdue payment. The government ban on the publication of the magazine was a continuing drain on *The Penny Dreadful*'s finances.

"I don't want to worry William with this, not yet. Besides, what can I really tell him? There are still more questions than answers."

For a moment the two of them sat there in silence, both trying to unravel the mystery. Penny's mind returned to the lecture room at the Society, remembering how Professor Röntgen's gaze had gleamed with a missionary zeal. *These rays are a phenomenon of the ether,* he had said. *Soon we will be able to harness their power to transcend the physical laws that bind us...*

Rising to her feet, Penelope plucked her parasol from where it was hanging on the coat stand.

"Where are you going?" Alfie asked, scrambling to his feet to follow her as Penny headed for the door.

"To find out more about Professor Röntgen's mysterious rays," she replied, glancing back over her shoulder. "I think it is time for a science lesson."

"I am no longer your tutor, Miss Tredwell," the man replied, peering intently at the contents of a bubbling test tube. "Your guardian, Mr Wigram, made that abundantly clear after that unfortunate incident when my demonstration of the combustible properties of calcium carbide ignited the curtains in your drawing room."

He bent over his scientific equipment again, using a pair of iron tongs to carefully place the test tube back in its ring stand, the Bunsen burner beneath emitting a hissing flame. His pale, pudgy face sweated with the act of concentration, peering intently through tinted spectacles to ensure the correct calibrations were made. He couldn't be more than thirty at most, but with his rumpled tweed coat and prematurely thinning hair he seemed somehow much older. A fountain pen was sticking out of his top pocket, the black ink from its leaking nib staining the cloth.

"But you were the finest tutor I ever had, Professor Walker," Penelope replied, resorting to flattery to try and wheedle from him the information she required. "It was only thanks to your quick thinking that you prevented the whole house from going up in flames. I could not imagine a more powerful demonstration of the destructive power of science."

Professor Walker glanced up unimpressed, well used to Penelope's wiles from the time he had acted as her personal tutor.

"And that is why I have been offered an assistant professorship here at the Royal College of Science. Although with the meagre wage they pay me, I doubt I will end up paying off the cost of those curtains before the year is out."

Penelope's face took on a sympathetic air.

"I am sure I could convince my guardian to waive this trifling bill," she reassured him. "Perhaps if you would indulge me with this enquiry, we could call this your final lesson and consider it payment in kind?"

Professor Walker narrowed his eyes, a calculating expression appearing behind his tinted spectacles.

"And perhaps some form of severance payment would be in order too?" he prompted. "To recompense me for the sudden nature of my dismissal."

"I am sure this can be arranged," Penny replied, holding the scientist's gaze.

With a sigh, Professor Walker reached forward to turn the gas tap, the Bunsen burner's flame dying away with a pallid glow.

"We have an agreement then, Penelope. Now, what exactly is it that you wish to know?"

With a glance towards Alfie, who was still peering at the bubbling test tube, Penelope tried to order her thoughts. There were so many questions she wanted to ask. How could a living man appear to walk through walls? What kind of chemical reaction could cause such a strange luminescence that a person's skin would glow green? Could the atoms that made up the solid matter of the universe be seemingly transformed into air? But Penelope knew that such esoteric enquiries would find short shrift with the practically minded professor. Instead, she asked the question at the forefront of her mind.

"What do you know of Professor Röntgen and

his X-rays?"

The scientist raised an eyebrow, absent-mindedly batting Alfie's hand away from the test tube as he commenced his explanation.

"The X-ray is an invisible form of radiant energy discovered by Professor Röntgen in 1895. He was experimenting with the transmission of electrical currents through a vacuum tube in his laboratory at the University of Würzburg, when he noticed a strange luminescence suddenly appear on a nearby screen. Investigating this phenomenon, he discovered that no matter what impediment he placed between the tube and the screen, the same shimmering image could be seen. These invisible rays – X-rays as he named them – could penetrate solid matter. Paper, wood, even metal. Only lead seemed to act as a block to their penetrative power."

The scientist scratched at his whiskers, bemused by his former pupil's pensive reaction.

"May I ask what the source of your interest in the X-ray is, Miss Tredwell? I was always under the impression that your preoccupations lay more with the arts than the sciences."

"I believe the worlds of science and fiction may be more closely related than previously suspected," she replied, absent-mindedly picking at a thread on her jacket as she mused on what she'd been told. "Have you not read the writings of H. G. Wells?"

"Bunkum and balderdash," the scientist replied with a snort. "I read his tale of *The Invisible Man* when it was serialised in *Pearson's Weekly*. The notion that a serious scientist would waste his time trying to render a man invisible was too risible for words."

Beneath her dark eyebrows, Penelope's gaze suddenly gleamed as inspiration struck. Professor Walker might find such a notion ridiculous, but what if a scientist of Professor Röntgen's calibre believed that there was a way to transcend the laws of nature? What lengths would he go to in the pursuit of his experiments?

"And what exactly is Professor Röntgen working on now?" she asked. "You said that he discovered the existence of X-rays in 1895. That was seven years ago. Surely he has made further discoveries since then."

Professor Walker shook his head.

"Röntgen's researches are a mystery," the scientist replied, carefully removing his spectacles and wiping them on his handkerchief. "He has not published a paper for nearly five years. At first he was recruited by the Kaiser to lead his scientific institute in Berlin, but then this year I heard that he had taken the chairmanship of the Society for the Advancement of Science right here in London. There have been rumours, of course, about his research. Some say that he is searching for more invisible rays as yet undiscovered by man. I very much doubt he will have much success."

With a dull pop, the contents of the test tube on the desk between them suddenly turned to a crimson shade. Professor Walker placed his spectacles back on to his nose.

"Now, if that answers your question, Penelope," he said, glancing down at his apparatus, "I must return to my experiments here at the Royal College. I look forward to receiving the letter from your guardian with my final salary payment."

"Thank you, professor," Penny replied as the scientist lit the Bunsen burner again. "It has been most illuminating."

XIV

"But I still don't understand how what Professor Walker told us can possibly help to free Monty."

Alfie shook his head, a perplexed expression lining his features as they turned left off the Strand, heading up Bedford Street back to *The Penny Dreadful*'s office. The late afternoon sun was already three-quarters of the way across the sky, weary office boys unbuttoning their cuffs as they left work to search for the nearest hostelry. Penelope squinted into the sunlight. At a newsstand on the corner, unnoticed by them both, a billboard proclaimed *The Evening Standard*'s headline:

CORONATION POSTPONED

"It proves there's a connection," Penny replied. "You heard what Professor Walker said. Röntgen was recruited by Kaiser Wilhelm to lead his scientific institute in Berlin. It was only this year that he made his way to London to join the Society for the Advancement for Science. Now all we have to do is find out how his experiments have created these radiant boys. Once we've proved that they were the ones responsible for the theft of the Crown Jewels, then Inspector Drake will have no choice but to release Monty."

The two of them were nearing the broad stone steps that led up to the offices of *The Penny Dreadful*.

"And how are we supposed to do that?" Alfie asked as they started to climb the steps. "If Professor Röntgen really is some mad scientist who has trained an army of ghostly thieves to do his bidding, then he's hardly going to let you waltz into the Society again to catch him mid-experiment."

Unable to answer, Penny reached for her keys.

"I don't know yet," she said, a cloud passing over her brow. Reaching for the door handle, she noticed that it was already unlocked; her guardian must have returned from the printers in their absence. Maybe Alfie was right, perhaps it was time to confide in William at last. Opening the door, her eyes widened in surprise at the sight that awaited her.

Seated behind her desk, his broad shoulders slouching forward as he rested his head in his hands, was Monty. The beginnings of the beard that Penelope had seen when she had visited him in his cell had now bloomed into full flower, dark shadows framing his features as he stared back at Penelope.

"Monty!" she cried, her face flushed with relief. "They've released you at last!"

But Monty's face remained grave as from the shadows on either side of the door two police constables appeared. Penny recognised them immediately as the same men who had dragged Monty from this office only days before. Her eyes darted around the room searching for the man who must have brought them here again. Inspector Drake stepped forward from the rear of the office, the expression on his face impenetrable.

"Have you released my uncle?" she said, addressing the question now to Inspector Drake.

The detective gave no reply. Instead he gestured through the open door to a waiting hansom cab parked on the street outside.

"You have kept us waiting for quite long enough, Miss Tredwell," he said. "My superiors have some urgent questions they wish to ask of you and your uncle. You must both accompany me at once."

As Alfie looked on anxiously, the burlier of the two police constables placed his hand on Penny's arm. His manner was respectful, but the meaning was clear. She had no choice in the matter. An avalanche of questions tumbled through her mind. Had Monty revealed the truth about his role at *The Penny Dreadful*? What further crimes had the Black Crow committed whilst she had been following his trail? And where on earth was her guardian when she needed him now?

"Am I under arrest?" Penelope asked, her gaze sparkling with defiance.

"No," Drake replied. "Not yet."

As Penny was escorted down the stone steps, she glanced back to see Monty, Inspector Drake and the second police constable keeping a tight grip on his arms as they shuffled down the steps. Beneath his new beard, the actor's face was pale, but meeting Penelope's gaze he managed to raise a weak smile.

"What about me?" Alfie asked, standing framed in the doorway.

"Consider yourself under house arrest," Drake snapped, not even bothering to glance back over his shoulder. "Stay here and if anyone calls at *The Penny Dreadful* for Montgomery Flinch, you take their details and tell them he is otherwise indisposed. I will return to question you anon."

As the burly constable held open the cab door, Penelope climbed inside. She glanced back to meet Alfie's gaze, recognising her own anxiety reflected in his eyes. Then Monty and the detective climbed up into the cab behind her, Drake drawing up the steps to leave his two constables standing on the pavement. With a rap of his knuckles against the roof of the cab, he signalled for the cab driver to depart. The cabbie twitched his reins to set his horses off at a trot, drawing the cab round in a sweeping manoeuvre as it headed back towards the Strand.

Alfie watched it depart with a sinking feeling. What would he tell Mr Wigram now?

"Where are we going?" Penelope whispered, sliding in her seat as the cab clattered round yet another corner.

"I don't know," Monty hissed, his bulky frame pressed against hers. "I'm just glad to be out of that blasted place."

The grand buildings of Whitehall flashed by the window: Admiralty House, Horse Guards, the Board of Trade; the great offices of state and government. It was clear to Penelope from the route they were taking that they weren't heading to New Scotland Yard. She glanced across at Inspector Drake, the surly detective leaning forward in his seat to fix them both with a belligerent glare.

"If I had my way, I would have left you to rot in that cell until you told me the truth, Flinch," Drake snapped, drumming his fingers to match the rhythm of the horses' hooves. "You're hiding something, that's for sure. However, events are moving too fast for me to wait for you to crack. It seems as though your niece's preposterous story might warrant further investigation after all." He turned towards Penelope. "And if I find out that you've been lying to me, girl, I'll put you into a cell right next to your uncle and let your age be damned."

Penelope didn't quail under the fierceness of his gaze, determined not to show any sign of weakness. If she was to have a chance of solving this mystery, she had to convince Inspector Drake and his superiors that what she had said was true.

"So where are you taking us then?" she asked.

Drake just grunted in reply as the cab swung right off Whitehall. Pulling at his reins, the driver slowed his horses to a trot, bringing the hansom cab to a halt outside a smart row of terraced houses. Turning in her seat, Penny looked through the window, her heart skipping a beat as she saw their destination.

A white number ten was fixed to a black front door, an iron knocker in the shape of a lion's head resting beneath this. Above the letterbox she could just make out the following words on the nameplate:

FIRST LORD OF THE **TREASURY**

"My God," Monty breathed, peering over her shoulder. "This is 10 Downing Street."

XV

Penelope sat primly in her chair, nervously smoothing the folds of her skirt as Monty fidgeted on the seat next to her. In front of them, Inspector Drake was pacing the room, his shabby shoes wearing a path across the lush green carpet. With his threadbare suit, the detective seemed somehow out of place amid the dark oak elegance of the small outer office. At a desk by the window, a hawkish-looking man glanced up from his papers, a look of irritation flashing over his features at the inspector's incessant perambulation.

The shrill ring of the telephone on the private secretary's desk caused both Monty and Penny to jump in alarm. Lifting the handset, the secretary held the telephone close to his ear, listening intently as the voice of the person speaking squawked through the receiver.

"Yes, of course, sir," he replied, nodding his head in earnest. "I'll send them in straight away."

Reverently placing the receiver back in its cradle, the man looked up to meet Drake's expectant gaze.

"The Prime Minister will see you now," he said, gesturing towards the green baize door. Inspector Drake turned back to Monty and Penelope, motioning for them to follow him with a chivvying gesture. Rising from her chair, Penny followed his instruction, a nervous sensation tying her stomach in knots. When Inspector Drake said his superiors had some urgent questions for them, she hadn't imagined that he meant the Prime Minister. With his hand on the door handle, the detective turned back to face her.

"Remember what I said, Miss Tredwell. You had better be telling the truth."

His warning given, Inspector Drake opened the door, ushering them both into the Prime Minister's study. With a sense of awe, Penelope cast her eyes around the room, quickly taking in her surroundings with an authorial gaze.

Along the entirety of one wall, floor-to-ceiling bookcases stretched, their dark oak shelves filled with thick leather-bound volumes, whilst on the other walls gilt-framed portraits of past prime ministers were hung: Sir Robert Peel, Pitt the Younger, Benjamin Disraeli. But the room was dominated by a large mahogany desk, behind which the current occupant of this post was seated: Lord Salisbury. Prime Minister of His Majesty's Government.

Glancing up from the papers scattered across his desk, Lord Salisbury's eyes blinked myopically as he focused his gaze on his visitors. His bald head shone in the sunlight slanting in from the window, whilst behind his unkempt beard, a troubled expression haunted his features.

"And who are you?" he growled, staring pugnaciously at the detective.

"Inspector Drake, Your Lordship. I have been investigating the theft of the Crown Jewels. It was after I took Mr Montgomery Flinch into custody that I learned—"

"Yes, yes." The Prime Minister gruffly waved the inspector into silence. He turned towards a second man, who was standing by the window, his slicked-back hair and drooping moustache revealing the profile of his nephew, the First Lord of the Treasury, Arthur Balfour. "Arthur has read to me your report on the progress of your investigation. Damned disappointing it is too."

Inspector Drake bristled at the criticism, but with the same instinct for self-preservation that served him so well as a detective, he now held his tongue as Balfour began to speak.

"So these are your prime suspects then?" he asked bluntly. "A potboiler author and his slip of a niece?"

"As I explained in my report, Mr Flinch has

displayed an unnatural knowledge of the theft of the Crown Jewels, even describing the crime in the pages of his magazine mere weeks after it took place. As for his niece, Miss Tredwell has made several unsubstantiated claims that may be linked in some way to the calamitous events of Monday night."

Penelope stared at the inspector, a puzzled frown creeping across her brow. There had been no mention in yesterday's newspapers of any calamity. Then a shiver ran down her spine, her thoughts returning to the flock of ghostly figures she had watched emerge from the bowels of the Society late on Monday night. Could the radiant boys have struck again?

"And I have read your report and thank you for it, Inspector Drake," Balfour replied courteously. He turned his gaze towards Monty and Penelope. "Now, if this is Mr Flinch and his niece, you can return to your duties at the Yard."

Open-mouthed, Drake stared at the politician, unable to believe he had been dismissed in such a peremptory fashion. Then, with a swift nod of his head, he turned to leave, casting Penny a final warning glance as he stepped out of the office, the door closing behind him with a click.

From behind his desk Lord Salisbury stared up at them both, his shoulders sloped as if worn down by the cares of office.

"So you're Montgomery Flinch, eh?" he said,

fixing Monty with a melancholy stare. "My wife used to read every one of your tales in *The Penny Dreadful*. Whilst I worked through my red boxes, she would be sitting there in her armchair, her attention rapt as she turned the pages." The Prime Minister's voice trailed away, Lord Salisbury staring towards the fireplace where an empty armchair was set. "How I miss you, my dear."

Balfour cleared his throat, the sound of his cough bringing the Prime Minister's attention back to the matter in hand.

"And what about this latest story of yours then, Flinch?" Lord Salisbury peered down at his papers again. "*The Thief Who Wasn't There*. How do you explain the fact that it describes the treasonous crime of which you have been accused?"

Monty blanched, the sense that his new-found freedom might be short-lived swiftly dawning on his face. His hand reached up to nervously smooth his freshly grown bristles, streaks of grey now showing amidst the black.

"It's a coincidence," he replied. "You have to believe me, Your Lordship. I swear I am an innocent man."

Penelope looked on, almost holding her breath, as Lord Salisbury held Monty's gaze. If the Prime Minister of England didn't believe him, what hope was left? Her thoughts flicked through the clues she had found: the anonymous letter, the radiant boys, Professor Röntgen, and the secret passage joining the German Embassy to the Society for the Advancement of Science. Inspector Drake's last words of warning echoed in her mind. *You had better be telling the truth*. The truth was all she had left now.

Stepping forward, Penny cleared her throat with a delicate cough.

"My uncle is telling the truth," she began. "The inspiration for the plot of *The Thief Who Wasn't There* was not his own."

Monty glanced across at Penny in surprise. After all that she had said, he hadn't expected that Penelope would give up *The Penny Dreadful*'s secrets so easily.

"For the past year, Montgomery Flinch's fictions have been absent from the pages of *The Penny Dreadful*," she continued, "as my uncle has been afflicted by an ailment of the mind that has made it impossible for him to write. He has suffered from a dearth of inspiration, his muse sadly absent, meaning that every story that he started failed to get past the first page."

Lord Salisbury stared at Penelope as she pressed on with her explanation, his expression inscrutable beneath his bristling eyebrows.

"This is why *The Penny Dreadful* launched a competition for its readers to suggest the plot for Montgomery Flinch's newest tale. Most of the entries he received were unworthy of my uncle's talent, but there was one letter that suggested a story based around a most audacious crime: the theft of the Crown Jewels from the Tower of London itself."

In the lengthening shadows of the Prime Minister's study, the three men listened spellbound as Penelope recounted the events that had brought her to this place. The anonymous letter signed with the sketch of a black crow, the sightings of the radiant boys spread across the city, the trail that had led her to the Society for the Advancement of Science and her suspicions about Professor Röntgen.

Unlike Inspector Drake, the two statesmen listened to her tale in silence, interrupting only to clarify a particular point or ask an illuminating question, and when she had finally finished speaking Lord Salisbury turned to his nephew, now standing pensively beside his desk.

"So what do you make of this, Arthur? If what Miss Tredwell says is true, then it confirms our worst fears."

"What do you mean?" Penelope asked, no time now for society's normal courtesies. In her mind she could see the two black-coated figures slipping through the shadows as she stalked them through St James's Park. "What has been stolen from Buckingham Palace?"

For a second, the politicians remained silent.

Then with a glance at the Prime Minister as if seeking his permission to speak, Balfour gave his reply.

"Not what, Miss Tredwell, but who," he said bluntly. "On Monday night, King Edward the Seventh was kidnapped from Buckingham Palace directly under the noses of his guards."

Penny and Monty gasped in unison, this revelation leaving them both reeling.

"And that's not all," Balfour continued. "The rest of the royal family are missing as well: Queen Alexandra, the Duke of York, Princess Victoria, the Duke of Connaught, the Duchess of Fife. Nearly thirty members of this nation's ruling family all spirited from their palaces and stately homes by persons unknown. At this very moment, Great Britain has no king."

Monty stared at the First Lord of the Treasury aghast. "But the coronation is tomorrow."

"The coronation has been postponed," Balfour replied soberly. "The press has been informed that the King is suffering from a digestive complaint, and that the royal family have withdrawn from all public duties out of respect for his condition, but we will only be able to maintain this deception for a limited time. We must find the King and restore him to his throne before Britain's enemies can act in our hour of weakness."

Penelope's mind raced, trying to join the dots between what Balfour had told them and the clues that she'd already found.

"Our enemies?" Monty asked. "Surely you don't mean the Boer? I thought that we'd finally seen the back of those blighters with the signing of the Treaty of Vereeniging."

Balfour shook his head.

"I am not thinking of our recent foes in Africa," he replied. "The Boers fought with guns, but the enemy we face now is of a more cunning mind."

Penelope remembered the naval uniforms that she had seen hanging next to the radiant boys' disguises. But before she had the chance to voice her suspicions, Lord Salisbury cleared his throat with a bone-rattling cough.

"My nephew has omitted to inform you of one fact. Not all of the royal family have been spirited away. Queen Victoria's eldest grandchild, Kaiser Wilhelm the Second, King of Prussia and Emperor of Germany, is in London for his uncle's coronation. If King Edward and his family have been murdered by these ghostly thieves you have seen, then the Kaiser is next in line to inherit the British throne."

Penelope stood there in silence, digesting the full meaning of the Prime Minister's words. If what Lord Salisbury said was true, then this was a conspiracy to unseat King Edward the Seventh and put Kaiser Wilhelm the Second on the throne in his stead. The British Empire conquered by Germany without a single bullet fired. She remembered the haunted features of the boy she had seen hiding in the shadows outside the palace, his skin glowing green as if lit from within. Did he realise the part he was playing in history?

"But if you know all this, why don't you search the German Embassy?" she asked. "I told you what I saw there. Perhaps the King and his family are hidden there too?"

"By God if I could," Lord Salisbury cried, slamming a fist against his desk before succumbing to a coughing fit. While he recovered himself, his nephew stepped in with his own explanation.

"The German Embassy is the sovereign territory of the Imperial Reich. If I even sent Inspector Drake or one of his men inside to follow this lead you have found, the Kaiser would be within his rights to treat it as a declaration of war."

Monty piped up in outrage.

"But if those blighters have taken dear old Teddie, then surely we can fight to find our King?"

Balfour set his face in a mollifying expression, even as Lord Salisbury beamed his approval at Monty's patriotic outburst.

"The situation is rather more delicate than that," he replied, steepling his fingers in front of him as he stepped forward to explain. "If it turned out that our suspicions were unfounded, the price we would pay for any rash act would be a high one. The Triple Alliance between Germany,

Italy and the Austro-Hungarian Empire would mean that the forces of half the continent would be lined against us. We cannot risk blundering into war on the strength of a young girl's word."

"So what do we do?" Penelope asked, an indignant blush colouring her complexion. "Wait for the coronation of Wilhelm the Second instead?"

Lord Salisbury shook his head with a growl.

"The British public would not wear it," he replied. "Such an event would mean the end of the monarchy, provoking civil unrest and protests in the street. The fabric of our nation would be torn to pieces and the great Empire that Queen Victoria built, God rest her soul, would fall to our enemies."

Balfour turned to Monty again.

"There is to be a reception at the German Embassy this evening – an Anglo-Germanic Commemoration to celebrate the achievements of both our great nations. The great and the good from London to Berlin will be in attendance – industrialists, writers, artists and scientists – and the guest of honour will be Kaiser Wilhelm himself. I will be attending as a representative of His Majesty's Government, but I would also like to extend an invitation to you, Mr Flinch, as one of this nation's greatest novelists."

"I would be delighted," Monty replied with a grin, the prospect of fine wine and canapés a welcome change from the slop he had been served at New Scotland Yard.

"And of course you will accompany your uncle, Miss Tredwell," Balfour said, turning now to Penelope. "I would like you both to act as the eyes and ears of our search for the King and the rest of the royal family. Anything you see or hear that raises your suspicions or could give a clue as to where the King has been taken, you must inform me immediately. We are facing a ruthless foe and must match their cunning with our own guile. There may well be dangers, but the very fate of our nation rests upon your success."

Monty paled as the convivial evening he had imagined was replaced in his mind by more dangerous entertainments, but Penny held her head high as she met the First Lord of the Treasury's gaze.

"My uncle and I will be proud to serve our country," she replied, her features set in a resolute expression. "We will find King Edward the Seventh and make sure he is back on his throne in time for the coronation."

XVI

Beneath an ornately painted ceiling showing a menagerie of beasts, Penelope stood alone in the midst of the reception, watching the dizzying whirl of guests as they thronged the ballroom. The grand space was almost overcrowded, every member of London society eager to partake of the Kaiser's hospitality, especially as the sad news of the King's illness had brought preparations for the coronation festivities to a premature end. Long lines of gaudily coloured flags were hung from the white and gold galleries; magnificent chandeliers with their tinted crystals illuminated festoons of flowers.

Uniformed waiters weaved their way through the crowd, the trays balanced on their hands filled with canapés of herring flakes, Bavarian blue cheese and spicy sausage. Looking around the ballroom, Penny saw faces familiar to her from the pages of *The Times*: artists and authors, politicians and musicians, industrialists and engineers. A smattering of military uniforms could be seen amidst the tailcoats and evening gowns, the top brass of Great Britain and Germany eyeing each other suspiciously over the canapés. The great and the good, Balfour had said, but glancing round the room the only women that Penelope could see were the wives and daughters of German diplomats, laughing coquettishly at the gallant remarks of their distinguished guests.

Beneath one of the grand chandeliers, Penelope could see that Monty had cornered one of the waiters; his wine glass was half-drained as he sampled the various German delicacies. From the ruddy sheen of his cheeks, it appeared that he had devoted more of the evening to supping the Kaiser's Riesling than to searching for clues of the King. Penny felt a hand on her shoulder followed by the rasp of a German accent.

"Ah, Madame Curie," the voice proclaimed. "We meet again."

Turning in surprise, Penelope found herself gazing up into the face of Professor Röntgen, the scientist fixing her with a penetrating stare.

"I'm afraid you must have mistaken me for somebody else," Penny replied, a slight tremor in her words. She turned to move away from the professor, her heart thudding in her chest at her discovery. Röntgen caught hold of her arm, his powerful grip keeping Penny in her place.

"Do not insult my powers of observation,"

the man hissed. "I recognised you from the moment I set eyes on you this evening. You are the busybody who sneaked into the Society yesterday, impersonating Madame Curie when the arrival of her train was delayed. Why are you meddling in my business and asking questions of matters beyond your imagining?"

He squeezed her arm, Penelope's faint cry of pain masked by the noise of the chattering guests.

"Who are you?" he hissed.

Penny winced, the scientist's tightening grip becoming more painful still. She could feel his fingernails pressing into her skin as if he was trying to dissect her with his bare hands. With a growing sense of fear, she stared up into his eyes; the fire that burned there was a pale imitation of the luminescence she had seen on the faces of the radiant boys.

"What do you know of my experiments?"

Penelope struggled, but Röntgen's grip was too tight. There was no way she could free herself without causing a scene. Her saviour came, though, from an unexpected source.

A sudden fanfare of trumpets turned the gaze of every guest to the front of the grand ballroom.

"My lords, ladies and gentlemen, his Imperial Majesty, Kaiser Wilhelm the Second."

Dressed in a Prussian-blue uniform, the German Emperor entered the room, flanked on both sides by his guards. His steely gaze swept across the ballroom, inspecting the guests gathered there as if they were soldiers assembled for parade inspection. Beneath the gold braid that decorated his shoulders, the Kaiser's chest was covered in more medals than material, the most glittering of these the Order of the Black Eagle hanging from a chain around his neck. As the Kaiser stepped on to a dais that had been set in front of a huge portrait of himself, a respectful hush settled over the room.

Penelope felt Professor Röntgen loosen his grip on her arm. There was no way he could risk a disturbance in the middle of the Kaiser's address.

The Kaiser stood there in silence, his expression stern as his left hand clutched the hilt of his sword. Forgetting for a moment the danger she was in, Penny stared in fascination at this regal figure she had only seen before in the pages of newspapers. His dark hair was slicked back in the military fashion, and the ends of his extravagantly waxed moustache stood to attention as well, its bristling spikes forming a W beneath his nose.

"My lords, ladies and gentlemen," the Kaiser began. "It warms my heart to see you all gathered here this evening. I am proud to come back to this land that my grandmother, Queen Victoria, ruled with such great dignity: the land of Shakespeare, Dickens and Flinch. Our two nations share a great heritage: scientific endeavour, artistic expression and, of course, our military might. We belong to the same great Teutonic race that Heaven has entrusted with the culture of the world. What other nation could match our accomplishments? Not the French," he spat. "Nor those upstart colonists in America who you so unfortunately misplaced."

Near the front of the audience, Penny caught a glimpse of Balfour as he listened intently to the Emperor's address; the First Lord of the Treasury was frowning at this last remark.

"As I said," the Kaiser continued, "we share a great heritage and a common destiny as well. Eighteen months ago as I sat by my dear grandmother's side, she beckoned me forward to hear her dying wish. 'Our two great nations should stand together,' she told me. 'Together we shall keep the peace of the world. You will make sure of that, won't you, my dear boy?'"

The German Emperor paused for a moment, dabbing his eyes as if moved by the memory. Then, seemingly recovering himself, he clicked his fingers imperiously, beckoning for a nearby waiter to bring him a glass of wine.

"Unfortunately my Uncle Bertie cannot be here this evening as I hear he has succumbed to a digestive disorder." In the audience, the British guests shuffled awkwardly, uncomfortable to hear their king spoken of in such a familiar way. "Whilst this may mean that the coronation is postponed, I hope that it will not be too long before your new King rises from the throne in Westminster Abbey."

His piercing blue eyes twinkled with a mischievous gleam as he raised his glass.

"But for now, I bid you to toast the eternal friendship that rests between us. To Germany and Great Britain – may the ties that bind us grow even stronger still."

The assembled guests raised their glasses in reply. "To Germany and Great Britain," they chorused.

Applause rang out as the Emperor stepped down from the dais, his aides ushering forward a cluster of handpicked guests to greet him. As an excited hubbub of conversation resumed around the room, Professor Röntgen redoubled his grip on Penelope's wrist.

"Now, I think we should continue our conversation in a more secluded setting," he hissed. But as the scientist turned to drag her through the throng, he found the figure of Monty blocking his path.

"There you are, Penelope!" Monty exclaimed, his wine glass now refilled. "A capital speech from the Kaiser, don't you think? It was almost enough to make me feel fond of our neighbours across the water." He lifted a sausage from the plate of a passing waiter and stuffed it into his mouth. "And this bratwurst is a delight!"

Noticing for the first time Professor Röntgen's hand on Penelope's arm, Monty brushed his own greasy fingers down the front of his dark tailcoat and then extended his hand in greeting.

"I don't think I've had the pleasure of making your acquaintance, sir. Please allow me to introduce myself. I am Montgomery Flinch – you may well know my stories from the pages of *The Penny Dreadful*."

Professor Röntgen glared at Monty's outstretched hand, the thwarted expression on his face revealing the scientist's frustration. He had no choice but to release his grip on Penny's arm, extending his hand to meet Monty's in a stiff handshake.

"I am Professor Wilhelm Röntgen," he replied. "And I am afraid that I am not familiar with this 'Penny Dreadful' of which you speak. I am a man of science, not a follower of the fripperies of fiction."

He broke off the handshake with a barely courteous nod, before turning his attention to Penelope again.

"Now, if you would care to accompany me, *Penelope*, we can resolve this matter without interruption."

Penny shook her head in reply.

"The matter is already resolved. As I have already said, Professor Röntgen, I believe that you have mistaken me for another." With a swish of her violet evening gown, she manoeuvred herself until she was standing by Monty's side. "Now, if you will excuse me, I am afraid I am feeling a trifle unwell." She took hold of Monty's arm, angling her face upwards to meet his gaze. "Uncle, would you be kind enough to take me outside for some air?"

"Are you sure that you don't just need some sustenance, my dear?" Monty asked, beckoning towards a passing waiter with a tray of canapés. "Perhaps a bite of this bratwurst will restore your spirits?"

Penny shook her head, waving the waiter away whilst Professor Röntgen watched her with a wolfish scowl.

"No," she replied faintly. "It is the atmosphere here that I find oppressive." She tightened her grip on Monty's arm, feeling him twitch as she pressed her nails in. "I would be most grateful if you could accompany me outside for a brief respite."

Hiding a wince behind his whiskers, Monty swiftly nodded his head.

"Of course, my dear," he replied with as much grace as he could muster. He turned towards Röntgen again. "Delighted to make your acquaintance, professor, but for now I must bid you *Auf Wiedersehen*! My niece Penelope has a delicate constitution and such a grand occasion as this is all rather overwhelming for one so young."

Penny fanned her face, her features a mask of innocence as Röntgen glared back at her. With a vexed growl, the scientist turned on his heel, heading back into the crowd of distinguished guests as Monty took Penelope's arm in his and steered her towards the door.

"Are you feeling quite yourself?" he asked as they swept a path through the swathes of Anglo-German aristocracy, their braying voices blending in a North Sea stew. "Didn't the Prime Minister ask us to act as his eyes and ears here to help track down the King?" Monty cast a mournful glance at a passing tray of wine and spirits, the brimming glasses just out of reach. "We can hardly do that if you ask to leave before the party is over."

Penelope glanced back over her shoulder, catching a glimpse of Professor Röntgen's electrified coiffure joining the throng of guests surrounding the Kaiser. As the German Emperor held forth, his face fiercely earnest, she spotted Balfour there too, a worried expression lining the politician's brow.

"Professor Röntgen recognised me," she replied, turning back as Monty led her through the crowded ballroom. "From my visit to the Society for the Advancement of Science next door." Penny glanced down at her bare arm, seeing the red marks of Röntgen's fingers there. "He said that I was meddling in matters beyond my imagining and demanded to know what I knew of his experiments."

"Hmmph," Monty grunted as they neared the grand doors overlooking the embassy's private garden. "He seemed a rather arrogant fellow to me."

Sidling past the last of the reception guests, Monty gestured for the guard standing sentry at the doors to open them to let them pass.

"My young niece is feeling a trifle unwell," he said, slowly enunciating every word as though he was speaking to a child. "I believe that a spot of fresh air in the garden will help her to recover herself."

Puzzled, Penelope glanced across at the guard as he turned to unbolt the doors. Her heart skipped a beat as she saw he was dressed in the same dark-blue naval uniform she had last seen hanging next to the clothes of the radiant boys. Its brass buttons glinted beneath the glow of the electric chandeliers, and as Penny's gaze tracked upwards to the sailor's face she feared she would see the same green glow that she had glimpsed in the shadows of St James's Park. The old sailor peered back at her with a look of concern, his ruddy features framed by a pair of mutton-chop whiskers. This was not one of the radiant boys.

Holding the door open, he let them both pass

with a respectful nod of his head, Monty ushering them out into the garden as the sun began to set behind the trees. Penelope shaded her eyes against the slanting rays. Before her, she could see a sight more graceful than the assembled elegance of the guests inside the ballroom: lush ferns and flowering shrubs, azaleas, rhododendrons and exotic trees; the splendour of the ambassador's walled garden taking her breath away. Instead of the empty chatter of conversation and clinking glasses, Penny could hear the sound of birdsong now; nature intruding on this square of London soil.

She shivered, goosepimples creeping across her bare arms as the evening chill descended. Noticing her discomfort, Monty turned back towards the door.

"Let me fetch you your shawl, Penelope. We don't want you to catch your death out here. I'll only be a moment."

Before Penny could protest, Monty had darted back inside the ballroom, his path to the cloakroom taking him past a passing tray of canapés. Through the window, Penny spied Professor Röntgen in conversation with the Kaiser, the two men standing apart from the throng. The German Emperor's brow was furrowed with a frown, and beneath the ridiculous topiary of his spiked moustache, his mouth was set in a thin-lipped scowl. From the animation of the scientist's gesticulations, she suspected that her presence there was the subject of their conversation.

Following a path leading between the herbaceous borders, Penelope hurried out of sight of the ballroom, the ornamental shrubbery shielding her from view. She could hear the sound of a water feature hidden in the depths of the garden, the twisting path leading her beneath a canopy of trees as the birds nesting above sang out a song of warning.

Penelope froze. Sitting in the shadow of the furthest ash tree, she saw the figure of a boy dressed in a dark-blue naval uniform. As the last slanting rays of sunlight illuminated his face, she saw with a shiver that it was same face she had glimpsed in the shadows of St James's Park. The radiant boy – now unmasked at last.

XVII

The boy was completely unaware of Penny's presence, a small notebook perched on his knee as he sat watching the starlings and sparrows gambol in the last rays of sunshine. With a pen in his hand, his eyes followed the birds, tracing their movements with unhurried strokes.

Emboldened by his absorption in his task, Penelope crept forward silently. The noise of birdsong in the branches above grew more animated as she stepped from the path, the nesting birds aware of her presence even if the young sailor wasn't. She took this opportunity to study him more closely, his pale features showing no hint of the eerie glow she had glimpsed in the park. The boy's lips pursed in concentration as he sketched the scene in front of him.

From the place where she was standing, Penny could just peek over his shoulder. As his pen moved across the notebook page, she could see a sketch of a starling take shape, black lines extending from the boy's pen to capture its tail as it twitched; the bird's pointed beak was illustrated with a finesse beyond even any of the artists that Penelope had commissioned. There could be no doubt about it. This was the author of the anonymous letter that had been sent to *The Penny Dreadful*. This was the Black Crow.

"Ah, there you are, Miss Tredwell!" Monty's booming voice made her jump in alarm. The starlings and sparrows launched themselves into the air, flocking together to take sanctuary in the trees. "Now, here is your shawl – I don't want Mr Wigram to accuse me of letting you catch a chill."

Glancing up at them in surprise, the young sailor scrambled to his feet, his fearful gaze flicking from Monty to Penny in turn. Penelope stared back at the boy. He looked scarcely older than Alfie, his dark-blond hair trimmed short in the naval fashion, whilst his wiry frame was tensed as if awaiting an order as yet unspoken.

"No need to stand to attention on our account, my boy," Monty said, stepping forward to drape Penny's shawl across her shoulders. "There's no harm in taking the weight off your feet for a while, especially on as fine an evening as this." He tapped his nose conspiratorially. "Don't worry, I won't tell the Kaiser."

The young sailor stared back at Monty, seemingly transfixed.

"It's you," he breathed. The boy's voice was surprisingly gentle, a faint accent marking each of his words. "Montgomery Flinch – you've come to help me at last."

For a brief moment, Monty's face glowed with pride at being recognised. Then his brow clouded as the last of the boy's words hit home.

"Help you?" he said, scratching his head in puzzlement. "I'm afraid I've just stepped outside for a moment to take the evening air with my niece here. If you are in need of assistance, I suggest that you call on your compatriots inside."

The boy shook his head with an unexpected vehemence, the shadows of the fading light lending his features a haunted expression.

"I need no help from my countrymen. It is their acts of cruel folly that drove me to seek out your aid, Mr Flinch." He stepped forward. "Do you really not know who I am?"

With an expression of mounting unease, Monty glanced across at Penelope, willing her to come to his assistance. She stared up into the young sailor's face, seeing the gleam of defiance that shone in his eyes. His handsome features were a far cry from the ghostly spectre she had last glimpsed in the shadows of Buckingham Palace. She turned towards Monty.

"This is the author of the anonymous letter – the one that inspired *The Thief Who Wasn't There*." Monty's eyes widened in surprise as she spoke, staring at the boy in disbelief. "This is the Black Crow."

For a second, the three of them stood there in silence. Faint peals of laughter from the ballroom and the birds chirruping in the trees were the only sounds that could be heard. Then, with a growl, Monty reached out to grab hold of the boy's naval collar.

"You!" he spat, his face flushed with anger. "You are the reason that I languished in that blasted cell for days! The things that they said – that I was a traitor to my own country – when all the time it was your words that had put me in that place!"

Penny tugged at Monty's sleeve to try and prise his hands free.

"Monty, please—"

The young sailor stood firm in the face of Monty's rage.

"I am sorry if the letter I sent caused the finger of suspicion to fall on you, Mr Flinch. That was never my intention, but I could see no other way of warning you of the conspiracy that was afoot. I am Sea Cadet Alexander Amsel of the Imperial German Navy and the only traitor here is me."

With an exasperated snarl, Monty released his grip on the boy's collar, turning on his heel in the direction of the ballroom.

"And you will pay for your treachery," he said. "When Balfour learns that I've caught the

Crown Jewels thief, the stain on my name will be removed at last, whilst you will have the chance to learn the meaning of British justice. If you are lucky, your youth might allow you to escape the gallows."

"Monty, wait!" Penelope's cry caused the actor to pause in his step. "We have to listen to what he has to say. Remember, it is not the theft of the Crown Jewels that has brought us here this evening, it is the fate of the King."

As Monty stood glowering behind her, Penny turned back to face the young sailor. Straightening his collar, Amsel's gaze flicked to her, the blaze of his blue eyes filled with some hidden torment.

"Thank you, Miss Tredwell," he said, his English impeccable. "I can see from your actions that it is true what they say about the British sense of fair play."

Penelope fixed him with a calculating look as if weighing the evidence in her mind.

"There's something I don't understand," she said finally. "If you stole the Crown Jewels, then why send a letter to my uncle confessing your crime?"

"Shame," Amsel replied, his head hung low. "I joined the Imperial Navy to serve my country, not sneak about like a thief in the night. My father served the first Kaiser and he taught me that the only glory that could be found in war was amidst the heat of battle when you faced an enemy who was worthy of your hate." He glanced up again to meet Penny's gaze. "I thought Great Britain was that enemy.

"You must understand, Miss Tredwell," he continued, "the poison that had been poured into my mind. Every day I had been told that the British were a parasite feasting on the riches of the globe. A country grown fat and complacent from the proceeds of Empire; a decadent nation now led by a fool of a king. Your ministers corrupt, your policemen incompetent – how could I trust my secrets to your authorities?"

In her mind, Penelope could see the pages of the British newspapers, their stories all feeding the same hatred of Germany. The young sailor turned towards Monty again, his blue eyes shining with a new passion.

"But when I read your stories, Mr Flinch, I saw for myself the lies I had been told. In the pages of *The Penny Dreadful*, I discovered a land filled with heroes: men of valour who dare to face the darkness that lurks beyond this mortal realm, and where scoundrels pay the price for their villainy. I have also heard tell of your own exploits, sir – how you solved the inexplicable Bedlam mystery, and even captured the phantom of the Theatre Royal." Amsel's gaze darkened again, a shadow passing across his face. "And I knew that only Montgomery Flinch would be able to save me from this nightmare that I found myself trapped in."

"But why write anonymously?" Penelope pressed him. "The only clue as to your identity is a sketch of a black crow?"

The young sailor's gaze darted nervously in the direction of the embassy, the clink of glasses and the chatter of conversation carrying through the trees.

"I was afraid," he replied simply. "If my letter had been intercepted and it was discovered that I was giving aid to the enemy, then my life would have been forfeit. I sketched the raven in the shadow of the Tower of London on the very night that we were all sent to steal the Crown Jewels. In German, my name *Amsel* means blackbird, so with this sketch I thought that the genius of Montgomery Flinch would be able to find me." He glanced up at Monty again. "And I was right."

Penelope frowned. She was growing weary now of how the fictional Flinch took the credit for her own endeavours.

"But why did you send only one letter?" She sighed in exasperation. "What did you possibly think that Montgomery Flinch could achieve with this?"

The German sea cadet furrowed his brow in reply.

"I thought that by exposing their plot in the pages of *The Penny Dreadful* I would put an end to it at last, but if anything it has only accelerated their scheme. I tried to write more letters – to warn you that their plans proceeded apace, but since the revelations in the paper they have been watching us all like hawks. As I have faltered, their suspicions have grown and now I have been excluded from any further missions until my loyalty to the Fatherland can be proved."

"I don't understand," Monty butted in. "You talk of plots and schemes and claim you stole the Crown Jewels from the Tower of London itself, but how on earth did you achieve such a feat?" He glared at Amsel's sallow complexion with a doubtful eye. "You're no galloping ghost, but flesh and blood just like Penelope and me."

Turning away from the embassy, Amsel's blue eyes gleamed in the gathering gloom.

"Let me show you," he said.

XVIII

Penelope trailed her fingers along the blackboard, the dusty lines that she left marking her path as she followed Amsel along the corridor. In his hand, the young sailor gripped his new-fangled torch, its flickering light casting strange shadows across the equations that had been chalked there. As they crept quietly across the tiled floor, Penny could feel a distant tremor beneath her fingers, a low buzzing sound growing slowly louder as they neared the end of the corridor.

"What is that infernal noise?" Monty muttered, pressing his fingers to his temple. "It sounds as if they have a storeroom full of wasps down here."

Penelope frowned. This was the same sound that she had heard throbbing through the brick walls of the Society only two nights before. Now, as the three of them skulked through the bowels of the building, she was about to uncover its source.

It had been easy enough to reach this point.

Sea Cadet Amsel's uniform and bearing had brought no questions as he escorted Monty and Penelope through the German Embassy. Giving the glittering ballroom a wide berth, he had led them to the same side room that Penelope had discovered by chance. Opening the wardrobe, she had seen the clothes of the radiant boys still hanging on their rails, but Amsel just brushed these to one side as he ushered them into the wardrobe, ignoring Monty's protests as he led them down into the darkness.

Now in answer to Monty's muttered question, Amsel glanced back over his shoulder. "That is the sound of the generator," he replied. "The spark that Professor Röntgen needs for his inhuman experiments."

Shining his torch, he illuminated a door at the corridor's end. Unlike the others that they had passed, this door was made from solid steel, the sign screwed into it written in a German script:

GEFAHR! WENN DAS ROTE LICHT LEUCHTET, BETRETEN VERBOTEN.

Next to the door, an electric lantern was fixed to the wall, two sliding panels of glass masking the bulb. One of these was coloured red, the other green.

"Are we not in London any more?" Monty grumbled. "What does this blasted sign say?"

"Danger," the German sailor translated. "When the red light is on, entry is strictly prohibited."

As Amsel opened the steel door with a grunt of effort, Penny noted with relief that it was the green panel that was currently slid into position, Professor Röntgen's presence at the reception seemingly preventing him from conducting any more experiments tonight.

The sailor flicked a light switch and, as this illuminated the room, Penelope stepped forward to join him, letting out a low gasp of surprise as she took in her surroundings. She was standing in a large chamber, larger even than the grand lecture room in which she had first set eyes on Professor Röntgen.

In the centre of the room, two rows of ten chairs were set in parallel lines and although their arrangement reminded Penelope of the theatre, the design of these appeared more suited to a Bedlam cell. Heavy leather straps hung from the armrests, whilst similar restraints were fixed to the foremost legs of each chair, their construction seeking to confine completely whoever chose to sit in them.

Above the chairs, an array of peculiarly-shaped glass tubes was suspended from the ceiling. Induction coils and uranium interrupters connected the tubes, whilst rubber-insulated cables ran from this apparatus along the ceiling and down the walls, skirting past the chairs to lead to a lead-lined box that stood facing them on the other side of the chamber. This mysterious box was over seven feet high and approximately the same width. A room within a room, but for what purpose Penelope could not say.

A sudden clattering sound caused Penny to turn in alarm. Her anxiety quickly turned to annoyance as she saw Monty peering inside a tall wooden closet, a lead-lined apron crumpled on the floor beside him. As he stooped to retrieve it, he glanced up apologetically.

"I thought there might be another way out of here," he said, placing the apron back on its hanger inside the closet. With a weary sigh, Penelope turned back to face Amsel.

"What is this place?" she asked him.

"It is a torture chamber," the young sailor replied, a look of animal pain in his eyes. "This is where Professor Röntgen turns men into ghosts."

At this statement, Monty closed the closet door with a shudder.

"What do you mean?" he enquired, eyeing the leather straps and restraints dangling from the chairs with a nervous air. "Is he some kind of Dr Frankenstein?"

"He is more of a monster," Amsel replied darkly. Then in a bitter voice he began to recount the events that had brought him to this place.

"I am a Sea Cadet on His Majesty's Yacht *Hohenzollern* – the pride of the German fleet. On the announcement of King Edward the Seventh's coronation, the Kaiser sailed for London and, when we berthed here, he selected twenty of the sea cadets to form a shore party to carry out a mission for the glory of the Reich. I made sure that I was chosen – eager to serve my Emperor at last." He shook his head angrily. "What a fool I was."

The young sailor glanced around the chamber, Penny following his gaze as he stared at the rows of empty chairs.

"This is where they brought us. Down into the depths of this laboratory, hidden away from human sight. I know why now, of course – they could not let anyone see the blasphemy that they would create here. We were the youngest of the ship's crew, more used to feeling the wind on our faces, now locked inside this airless place while the light outside glowed red." He turned back to face Penelope, his eyes glistening as he relived the memory. "Professor Röntgen inspected us like laboratory rats – probing and measuring us, even connecting our bodies to strange machines that listened to our blood. And then when he was finally satisfied as to our fitness for his experiment, he instructed us to sit in these chairs that you see here."

With an absent-minded gesture, Amsel rubbed

his wrists as if he could still feel the straps chafing his skin.

"He said it wouldn't hurt," he said sullenly, his voice dropping to a low whisper, more like a child than a sailor of the Imperial German Navy. "He said that the straps were there to protect us." He stared up at Penny, his eyes black with betrayal. "He lied."

Amsel fell silent for a moment, as if the memories flickering across his features were too painful to express. Penelope held his gaze, seeing the depths of suffering that lurked there.

"What happened to you?" she asked, her own voice an echoing whisper.

"Once Professor Röntgen had made sure that the straps were secure, he retreated inside that lead-lined box to throw the switch that would bring his infernal machine to life." Amsel raised his gaze to the curious arrangement of tubes above their heads. "There came a sudden buzzing sound like thousands of bees hammering at the glass, but all I could see was the light glowing green." His hands trembled, reliving every moment of the experience again. "And then I felt the pain."

"It could only have lasted moments, but it felt like a lifetime. It was as though the room was flooded with an invisible fire. I heard the screams of my comrades, too painful to bear – my fellow sea cadets reduced to snivelling wrecks in mere seconds. As the buzzing ceased and the luminescent glow slowly faded from the glass, I looked down at my skin to see the same radiant fire running through my veins." He lifted his hand in front of his face. "Panicking, I tried to free myself and somehow found that I could slip from the restraints that held me without a struggle. I saw my comrades do the same, their limbs melting through the leather straps as they hauled themselves upright, every face a glowing green mask of pain."

Penelope and Monty listened aghast, the faint buzz of the generator the only sound that could be heard as the young sailor continued his story.

"When Professor Röntgen emerged from the safety of his antechamber, he clapped his hands together in delight. 'It worked!' he cried, his dark eyes ablaze as we stood there with a living fire burning in our veins. Then he told us what he had done to us – how his machine had made us into ghosts of men.

"From this moment on, we were kept prisoners in this laboratory – unwilling subjects for the professor's endless experiments. At first, their effects only lasted for mere minutes – the strange glow quickly fading from our skin – but as Professor Röntgen tinkered with his infernal equipment the effects endured for longer with every experiment. We listened in fear as he increased the voltage of the electrical current and knew that when he next flicked the switch the pain would be even worse than the last time. I watched my friends, their touch turned to living fire as they tried to control this curse that had been cast upon us."

Amsel turned to face Penelope, his glistening gaze unable to disguise his distress.

"Professor Röntgen said that we alone were young enough to bear the strain of his experiments. That on the Kaiser's orders, he was transforming us into the ultimate fighting machine. Under his tutelage, he showed us how we could use our minds to control this accursed gift and then sent us out across London to carry out the Kaiser's commands: spying on government papers in Whitehall, stealing the Crown Jewels, even kidnapping the King."

Before Amsel could explain further, the distant sound of footsteps echoed from the corridor outside.

"Quick," he said, turning in alarm. "Someone is coming."

Penelope looked around in desperation, no sign of any place to hide as the footsteps echoed ever closer. She could hear the sound of German voices: the low rumble of Professor Röntgen's words answered by the clipped tones of the Kaiser. Amsel paled, their discovery imminent.

With a low whimper of fear, Monty clambered inside the closet. With fumbling fingers he wrapped himself in the folds of the aprons hanging there in a desperate attempt at disguise. Monty's bulk meant there was no room for Penny to hide there as well, the actor meeting her gaze with a shame-faced look of apology. Darting forward, she closed the closet door on Monty with a click and then turned to try to find her own hiding place.

"How about the box?" she hissed, catching hold of Amsel's arm to gesture to its lead-lined walls.

The young sailor shook his head, his own gaze desperately searching for sanctuary.

"If Röntgen is here to perform his experiments, then that is the last place we should hide." He dragged Penny towards a packing crate, standing in the shadows of the antechamber. "This was used to transport equipment from the *Hohenzollern*." Lifting the lid, he gestured for her to climb inside. "It is our only chance."

There was no time for Penelope to argue, the nearing voices announcing their imminent arrival. She clambered inside the packing crate, covering herself with the heavy blankets left as ballast at the bottom of the case. Then the young sailor climbed in beside her, silently drawing the lid of the crate over them both as the sound of footsteps entered the room.

They crouched there together, uncomfortably close, not even daring to breathe. Turning her head, Penelope peered through a crack in the packing case, trying to make out the identities of the figures still entering the room. She could see Professor Röntgen's rail-thin frame, his upright mane of unruly black hair dwarfing the figure of his Emperor. The Kaiser's personal guards stood sentry behind him, Wilhelm's lip curling in satisfaction as a platoon of black-coated boys marched into the room.

"*Zurück zu Ihren Posten!*" he barked. "*Ihre letzte Mission für den Ruhm des Deutschen Kaiserreiches ist es, die Britische Krone gefangen zu nehmen.*"

Penelope's grasp of German was even worse than her French, the Emperor's words holding no meaning for her.

"What is he saying?" she murmured softly, angling her mouth towards Amsel's ear in the cramped confines of the packing case.

"Their final mission," the sailor replied, his own voice barely a whisper, "is to capture the British throne for the glory of the Imperial German Empire."

Turning back, Penelope watched as the radiant boys saluted in reply and then marched to take their places in the empty chairs. Next to her, she felt Amsel stiffen with fear, but her own heart pounded with anticipation. Now she would see for herself the secrets of Röntgen's invisible rays.

But Penelope's sense of excitement was short-lived, as through the crack in the crate she saw the professor approach the store cupboard where Monty was hiding. She heard the sound of its door opening followed by a guttural exclamation.

"*Ach du meine Güte!*"

The Kaiser's guards rushed forward as Röntgen fell back in surprise, Monty emerging from the closet with a sheepish smile.

"Ah," he said, glancing nervously at the armed guards. "I appear to have taken a wrong turn. Would one of you gentlemen be kind enough to point me in the direction of the Emperor's reception?"

XIX

"It is him!" Professor Röntgen exclaimed as the guards seized hold of Monty. "The man I was telling you about, Your Highness." Röntgen peered inside the dark cupboard, pulling back the aprons hanging there to reveal its furthest recesses. "But there is no sign of the girl." He turned back to face Monty. "Where is she?"

"Steady on," Monty protested, struggling to maintain his composure as the Kaiser's guards held him captive. "There is no need to treat an honoured guest in this way. Surely, sir, you remember me from the reception?"

"I remember you," Professor Röntgen replied, meeting Monty's gaze with a suspicious stare. "But what are you doing in my laboratory and where is your niece?"

From her hiding place, Penelope held her breath, fearful that he would give them all away.

"My niece Penelope was feeling rather unwell," Monty replied. "I escorted her outside to hail a hansom cab, tipping the driver handsomely to return her home safely. But when I attempted to return to the reception, I think I must have taken a wrong turn and, after all manner of diversions, I found myself in this place." He wrung his face into a grateful smile. "Thank goodness you have found me."

The Kaiser stepped forward, his upturned moustache quivering with outrage.

"Do you really expect me to believe this, Mr Flinch? I am not one of your credulous readers. Now, tell me," he said, clutching the hilt of his sword with a malevolent air. "What really brought you here this evening?"

Monty quailed in the face of the Kaiser's iron glare.

"I swear that I found my way here by mistake," he insisted. "But I must admit that when I found this laboratory, I was somewhat intrigued. My compatriot, Mr Herbert George Wells, has had great success of late with his stories of scientific romance, and I saw here the chance to find my own inspiration. When I heard your footsteps approaching, I was unsure as to how my trespass would be received, so I took the precaution of hiding myself in this wardrobe." Monty raised his gaze to the array of gleaming tubes and coils suspended above their heads. "I so wanted to see what wondrous discoveries you have made here, professor."

Professor Röntgen scowled darkly at Monty's impertinence, but the Kaiser just laughed out loud.

"Your audacity astounds me, Mr Flinch – if only more of your compatriots had the daring you have shown, then Britain would not be in need of a saviour to restore the greatness that my grandmother bestowed. We will have to furnish you tonight with the inspiration you require for your astounding tales."

He turned to Professor Röntgen, the scientist now slipping a lead-lined apron around his neck. "Please explain to Mr Flinch the nature of the discoveries you have made, *mein Professor*."

"Are you quite sure, Your Highness?" Röntgen replied, glancing up at the Kaiser in surprise. "If my discovery was to be revealed in the pages of this 'Penny Dreadful' magazine..."

"Do not question me!" the Kaiser snapped in a sudden burst of anger. Then, recovering his composure almost as quickly as he had lost it, he spoke again in a more measured tone. "It will soon be time for the world to learn of the magnitude of our achievements as we enact the final stage of my master plan tonight. Mr Flinch may as well have the privilege of being one of the first."

An arrogant smile crept across the Kaiser's face. "And besides, I do not think he will have the chance to betray our confidence."

At the Kaiser's words, Monty looked nonplussed, but Professor Röntgen nodded his obedience, gesturing upwards towards the apparatus suspended from the ceiling.

"You see here, Mr Flinch, my own unique invention, the product of many years of research and countless experiments. This is the Röntgen Ray Generator – an X-ray machine like no other."

"Aren't X-ray machines rather old hat now?" Monty replied, glancing nervously at Röntgen's machine. "A circus trick allowing the curious to photograph the bones beneath the skin, but of little practical application."

The scientist bristled at Monty's off-hand dismissal of his life's work.

"You do not understand the true potential of these invisible rays that will soon take my name. Imagine if the X-ray could be manipulated, not merely to take shadow photographs but to transform the human body into its shadow form. The flesh imbued with the same penetrative power that the X-rays themselves possess – the power to pass through solid matter without any harm."

Monty laughed nervously. "I'm afraid your proposition is too far-fetched, professor – even for the pages of *The Penny Dreadful*. I can see that I will have to seek inspiration for my next tale elsewhere. Now, if you would please excuse me—"

"Stay where you are," the scientist hissed, the Kaiser's guards tightening their grip on Monty's arms. "What I am telling you is true!

"After my discovery of the X-ray, I became convinced that its remarkable power could in some way be harnessed to challenge the laws that govern the natural world. These rays are able to seep through all manner of matter – wood, stone, metal and more – their penetrative power is without parallel. Through a process of careful experimentation, I discovered a means by which I could manipulate their creation and thus harness their power. Using the application of radiation to their generation, I found that I had created a completely new form of invisible ray: no longer merely X-rays, but now radioactive Röntgen rays with the power to transform living beings into ghosts who can walk through walls."

Monty gasped in fear but, ignoring his reaction, the professor pressed on with his explanation.

"When the Röntgen rays are fired directly at a living man they have the power to transform his constitution as the atoms that make up the physical body are saturated with their penetrative power. Drawing on Dr Jackson's research into how electrical impulses from the brain control a subject's movements, I discovered that the effects of these Röntgen rays could also be controlled by the power of thought. With the application of his own mind, a subject can momentarily loosen the bonds that hold the very atoms of his body together, allowing him to pass through any object unharmed."

Professor Röntgen glanced at the men seated beneath his machine. "The mental effort required to control this strange power is quite considerable, but fortunately with His Majesty's support I have the fittest of subjects for my experiments."

The Kaiser fixed Monty with a malevolent stare, seemingly enjoying his discomfort.

"Do you see what this means, Mr Flinch? With this power at my command, the German Empire will be invincible. My armies will be able to march through a hail of bullets and bombs without harm, my naval ships will steam through any blockade unhindered; no nation's defences will be able to resist the strength of my New Atomic Army."

Monty paled, tiny droplets of sweat beading his forehead. "You talk of war," he said. "There is no way Great Britain would allow it."

"Great Britain is already mine," the Kaiser roared, rattling his sabre with his withered hand. "Once my troublesome uncle is disposed of, there will be a new King on the throne and I promise you that my reign will be a glorious one."

He turned again to Professor Röntgen, who was poised at the entrance to the antechamber. "Now, let us not delay any further; the tide will soon be turning and these young men must be prepared for their final mission."

With an obedient nod, the scientist hurried inside the lead-lined box. There came the sound of switches being flicked followed by a humming noise slowly rising in volume.

"Your Majesty," Röntgen called out. "I think it would be prudent if you joined me inside this protective shield."

With a nod to his guards to follow him, the Kaiser retreated to the antechamber's interior, its lead-lined door slamming shut once Monty had been dragged inside. The humming sound grew louder still as the coils of the Röntgen Ray Generator began to crackle into life.

Hidden inside the cramped confines of the packing crate, Penelope listened in fear. The giddy whine of the generator was reaching a crescendo and, through a crack, she could see the suspended glass tubes begin to glow with a flickering green light. She felt Amsel's hand clutch her own.

"Be brave," the boy whispered. "You must steel your mind against the pain."

Penelope stared up at the strange apparatus. With a snapping sound, electrical currents shimmered from its coils, passing through the uranium interrupters as the invisible rays surged through the long glass tubes. She watched spellbound as a yellowish-green light spread over their surface in a rolling, cloud-like wave; the eerie luminescence growing stronger with the snapping of the discharge.

Beneath the machine, the radiant boys were bathed in the same glowing green light, their expressions frozen in pain as the rays shone through.

Penelope closed her eyes against the horror, but the uncanny light was imprinted on her retina; the indelible image of a coiled green snake slithering inside her mind. She felt a burning sensation pulse through her veins, and as Amsel's body twisted in the narrow space next to hers, she knew he felt the same. The pain was almost unbearable; a soul-searing torment transforming every atom of her being. Biting her lip to try and stifle her own cry, Penny tasted blood on her tongue, the clamour of pain reaching a crescendo as she slowly slipped into oblivion.

From the ceiling, the crackling whine of the Röntgen Ray Generator snapped into silence, the iridescent glow slowly fading from its long glass tubes. But beneath these, the radiant boys were rising from their chairs, the features of every single cadet a vivid glowing green.

With Professor Röntgen by his side, the Kaiser emerged from the lead-lined antechamber, Monty still struggling in the clutches of the guards as they dragged him back into the laboratory.

"My Lord," he murmured, staring in horror at the shining features of the radiant boys. "What have you done to them?"

"They have been transformed," the Kaiser replied, his blue eyes sparkling with delight. "It is a shame that you will not be able to write this tale of the triumph of science."

"What do you mean?" Monty asked, blanching in fear as the guards released him.

Ignoring his question the Kaiser turned to address the cadre of radiant boys.

"Take him with you to the Tower," he barked. "Dispose of him in the same dungeon that my uncle calls home. The *Hohenzollern* will sail with the tide and you must return there with my precious royal cargo before we raise anchor."

The radiant boys raised their arms in salute, stepping forward as Monty shrank back in terror.

"No, please! I beg of you—"

Monty's protest curdled into a cry of anguish as the radiant boys seized hold of him, their glowing green fingers causing the actor to faint. Pulling their scarves across their faces, the black-coated figures dragged him from the room, the Kaiser and his guards following close behind.

With a last look around his laboratory, Professor Röntgen hurried to the door. Stepping outside, he reached up to the electric lantern that was fixed to the wall, sliding the green panel of glass into position in place of the red. Then the scientist pulled the door shut with a clang, turning his key with a click to keep the secrets of the Röntgen rays safely locked away.

XX

Penelope was lost in a darkling fog, fragments of memories fighting free from the cloaking mist that held her in its grip. She saw Monty quailing in front of the Kaiser, heard the whine of Professor Röntgen's impossible machine, watched as an army of radiant boys marched through the laboratory; but every time she tried to fit these memories into place, the darkness claimed them again.

Penny felt a distant thrum, a strange vibration that slowly dragged her out of the darkness and towards a glowing green light. As she neared it, she felt a burning sensation pulse through her veins again, the pain a pale shadow of what she had felt before. Taking a shuddering breath, Penelope opened her eyes to find herself staring into the face of a ghost.

She scrambled backwards in alarm, the train of her evening gown catching beneath her heel. Amsel rushed to her aid, little realising that he was the cause of her consternation, the young sailor's visage glowing as if lit from within. Penny stared down at her hand, the pulsing veins sketching a tracery of fire across her skin.

"What has happened to me?" she murmured, her memories slowly resurfacing out of the darkness. "What has he done to us?"

"He has made us into ghosts," Amsel replied, staring down at his own hands in disgust. "Do not worry, Miss Tredwell, the effects of Professor Röntgen's rays are still only temporary. Within a few hours, this strange fire you can feel racing through your veins will be gone, but we have to act now before it is too late."

Penelope glanced around the laboratory.

"Where's Monty?" she said. "Where have they taken him?"

"The same place where they have King Edward the Seventh and his family imprisoned," he replied. "The Tower of London."

Penny scrambled to her feet, shucking the naval coat that Amsel had draped around her shoulders to the floor. Hurrying to the steel door she turned the handle, only to discover that it was locked.

"We're trapped," she said, turning back to Amsel in dismay. "There's no way out."

The young sailor shook his head, picking his coat from the floor to drape it around Penny's shoulders again.

"No locked door can hold us now," Amsel

replied, reaching down to offer Penelope his hand. She stared down at his luminous fingers, the burning sensation pulsing through her flesh giving her own skin the same eerie glow. "It is all a matter of control," he told her. "The mastery of mind over matter – you must believe that you can walk through steel unscathed."

As the fire raced through her veins, Penny took hold of the boy's hand. Their shining fingers entwined with a sensation like lava melting, and then they stepped forward as one, their bodies slipping through the surface of the door as if it was made of water. Penelope felt her mind whirl, her brain refusing to believe the sensations that were pulsing through her frame. The world burned with the same fire that consumed her from within, her body vibrating in time with the billions of atoms that surrounded her. And then they were on the other side, Penelope untangling her fingers from Amsel's before turning back to stare at the steel door in disbelief.

"We did it," she breathed. "We walked through solid steel."

Amsel nodded, the expression on his face still grim. "We will have to walk through more than steel before the night is out," he replied, the lantern light outside the laboratory door reflecting the green glow of his skin.

For Penelope, the next few minutes passed as if in a dream, the two of them slipping through the corridors of the Society. No wall or locked door was a bar to their progress. Escaping through the tradesmen's entrance, they quickly ascended the steps to the pavement above, scurrying past the Duke of York statue before descending the stone steps that led to the Mall.

"We must hurry," Amsel said, keeping to the shadows as they rushed down the street. "The Kaiser and my compatriots have a head start and if they reach the Tower before us, then this British Empire of yours will be lost for good."

"I cannot keep up with your pace," Penelope gasped, the folds of her evening gown gathered in her grasp. "Not in these heels."

"Then what do you suggest?"

Penelope stepped out of the shadows, raising her hand to flag down a passing hansom cab.

"What are you doing?" Amsel hissed as the cab driver reined his horses to a halt.

With her face covered by the high collar of her borrowed jacket, Penny stepped up onto the cab's footplate.

"Making time," she replied, beckoning for Amsel to follow her. "You see, I know the power of fear."

"Where to, miss?" the cabbie asked, glancing back over his shoulder as Amsel and Penelope settled into their seats. Penny turned down the collar of her jacket to reveal her glowing green visage.

"The Tower of London," she replied with a hiss. "And don't spare the horses."

With a terror-stricken gasp, the driver shrank back in his box seat. He raised his whip with a crack, fear lining his features as he spurred the horses into life. The hansom cab jolted forward, throwing Penny and Amsel back in their seats, its wheels gathering speed as it headed for the river.

XXI

"This is an act of war," the voice boomed, its echo reverberating through the dripping walls. "I demand that you release my family at once."

From the darkness of the catacombs, Penelope craned her neck to see the figure of King Edward the Seventh clutching the bars of an iron cage. The long shadows cast by a flickering lantern glow revealed his Queen and the rest of the royal family standing huddled behind him, all held prisoner in the same sprawling dungeon. In front of the cage, the black-coated figures of half a dozen radiant boys could be glimpsed, the eerie gleam of their features still masked behind swaddling scarves.

By Penelope's side, Amsel shook his head in defeat.

"We're too late," he murmured. It seemed that the fear of God Penelope had struck into the heart of the hansom cab driver hadn't been enough to get them here in time.

After the trembling driver had deposited them at the bottom of Lower Thames Street, they had scurried past the shadows of the Tower, Amsel taking Penelope's hand in his own as they plunged into solid stone. Penny's mind reeled with every step they took, slipping through the walls of the Tower with a giddying sensation. She caught glimpses of roosting ravens, spiral staircases, scarlet uniforms standing sentry in the shadows; every snatched glance a brief respite before she was submerged again into solid stone. They were like ghosts, their passage undetected as they descended through the depths of the Tower before finally reaching this subterranean vault, long forgotten about by those above.

The sound of a cough echoed through the catacombs and then the figure of the Kaiser stepped through the gloom. His military greatcoat was buttoned to his neck, whilst the Imperial State Crown added precious inches to his height. Wilhelm the Second came to a halt in front of the cage, peering in at the King with a devilish smile.

"Come now, Uncle Bertie," he chided him. "It can hardly be an act of war if I am to sit on Britain's throne. Let us call this what it really is – a restoration of this nation's true heir. It is what my dear grandmother wanted, you know. A strong ruler to safeguard the Empire that she built, rather than a prancing peacock like you."

Facing his nephew, the King's features flushed with rage.

"How dare you, you trumped-up little pipsqueak!" the King roared. "My mother wanted no such thing!"

The Kaiser pouted in reply.

"Remember that I was there when she died," he snapped, stepping forward until he was standing almost next to the bars. "As I cradled her in my arms, I swear that she said with her dying breath that I should be King in your stead."

Thrusting his hands through the bars of the cage, Edward seized hold of the Kaiser's lapels. "You're a liar, Willie! You take that back this instant or I swear to God I'll thrash you to within an inch of your life."

As the Kaiser spluttered in reply, two of the radiant boys standing guard reached out to pull the King's hands away; the sight of their glowing fingers caused Edward to fall back with a cry of alarm.

Straightening his stolen crown, the Kaiser stared down at his uncle with a withering look.

"You are hardly in a position to make such threats," he sneered. "And it is lucky for you that I know the meaning of mercy, Uncle Bertie. If I had wanted to I could have sent my men to assassinate you in your sleep, rather than merely stealing the Crown Jewels to put a stop to your coronation – do not worry, these baubles will be much safer in the throne room of my Berlin Palace. And if you had agreed to sign the abdication papers renouncing your claim to the throne, then I would have been prepared to let you see out your days at Sandringham. There you would have been able to amuse yourself with your racing pigeons and other such diversions in your dotage."

Princess Victoria bent to her father's aid, cradling him in her arms. In the flickering glow of the lantern light, the King's features appeared deathly pale against the violet of his daughter's velvet gown. Behind them in the cage, the rest of the royal family stood powerless: the Duke of York stroking his moustache in an agitated manner, whilst Princess Louise silently sobbed. Clutching her grandchildren to her skirts, Queen Alexandra stared at the Kaiser with a cold fury.

"But as it stands," he continued regardless, "I will have to send you and the rest of your family into exile. I have the perfect home for you in mind – a comfortable manor house in the forests of Prussia, far enough away from the heart of the Empire to keep you all out of mischief."

"You will not succeed," the King gasped, slowly rising to his feet again. "The British army will fight to the death for its King."

"My scheme has been conceived to dispense with any unnecessary bloodshed," the Kaiser replied coldly. "When I became Emperor, my generals presented me with countless papers, maps and intelligence reports detailing this island's defences and setting out plans for invasion. With my dear grandmother still on the British throne, I would not countenance such a move, but after her death I returned again to consider their invasion plans. What I found was a recipe for disaster. Although it was clear that the might of the Imperial German Army could easily conquer this island, with the strength of your navy every possible invasion route was fraught with danger, with no guarantee that my troops would even make harbour. And what was worse, any act of aggression on my part could be the spark that would set the continent ablaze, drawing France, Russia and countless more nations into a bloody war with no clear prospect of victory."

The Kaiser's eyes gleamed with a steely light.

"As you know, dear Uncle, I pride myself on being a man of peace. So instead, I conceived this scheme to conquer your nation without a drop of blood spilled. By removing your sorry self and all other obstacles ahead of me in the line of succession, it will be my *bloodline* that delivers me the throne."

"This is intolerable," the King gasped, slowly rising to his feet again. "The British people will not stand for such skulduggery – let alone accept the sight of Kaiser Bill on the throne."

The Kaiser shook his head, the corners of his

mouth turning upwards in a mocking smile that matched the shape of his moustache.

"The British people will rejoice at the news," he replied. "I will oversee the unification of our two great nations and then take my rightful place on the throne as King Wilhelm – the first Emperor of the Imperial Anglo-Germanic Empire. With our armies and navies joined, I will be able to impose a lasting peace across the globe – by force if any nation dares to challenge me." He gestured to the phalanx of radiant boys forming a guard of honour behind him. "And with the soldiers of my New Atomic Army, I will restore your upstart colonies such as the United States of America to the bosom of the Empire again. Your British people, dear Uncle, will revere me as their saviour: the King who returned Great Britain to her rightful place in the sun. Grandmother would be so proud of me."

As King Edward seethed, the Kaiser turned on his heel.

"We can continue this discussion on the voyage to Prussia. I have prepared the guest suites on the *Hohenzollern*. My guards will return to escort you to the ship once I have taken my final leave of this city before I return as its King."

As the Kaiser spoke, two of the masked radiant boys dragged the bulky figure of a man through the shadows of the vault, the long tails of his dinner jacket scraping against stone. With a shiver of recognition, Penelope saw this was Monty, the actor's glazed eyes set in an unseeing stare.

With a jangle of keys, the first of the guards unlocked the iron cage. As the young children sobbed into Queen Alexandra's skirts, the rest of the royals backed away fearfully. The masked figures unceremoniously dumped Monty in a heap, his unconscious form slumped in the far shadows of the cell.

"In the meantime, Mr Montgomery Flinch will keep you company," the Kaiser called over his shoulder as the guards locked the cage again. "Although I fear he is hardly in a fit state to recount for you one of his entertaining tales."

Queen Alexandra's clipped voice cut through the funereal gloom.

"What have you done to him, you odious little man?"

Scowling, the Kaiser halted his step, glancing back with a thunderous expression on his face.

"Mr Flinch made the mistake of prying too closely into the affairs of state. It is only fitting that he now spends the rest of his days in this dungeon where so many traitors have languished before him." He narrowed his gaze, fixing the Queen with a savage glare. "And I would remind you to watch your tongue, Aunt Alexandra. After all, I will soon be your King." Drawing his greatcoat around him, the Kaiser turned again to leave. "I suggest that you ready your family for the journey ahead. The *Hohenzollern* sails with the tide."

Forming an escort around their Emperor, the radiant boys brandished their lanterns against the subterranean gloom; the next King of England guarded by a company of grey-green ghosts. As they marched in step through the catacombs, the light from their lanterns swept past Penelope's hiding place. Fearing discovery, she felt Amsel's hand close around her own as he pulled her back into the shadows. Focusing her mind, Penny felt her flesh seep through the stone walls of the dungeon, their bodies melting into the darkness until only their eyes remained. Unnoticed, Penny and Amsel looked on as the Kaiser and his guards passed by.

As the sound of their footsteps faded away, Penelope stepped forward again, her mind spinning as she peeled herself free from the stone. She could feel the very atoms of her being still pulsing with Röntgen's invisible rays, the sensation leaving her breathless.

"Where are they going?" she asked, peering into the darkness as the tread of the Kaiser's men faded into silence. Amsel emerged from the shadows, his face still lit from within by the same unearthly light that illuminated Penelope's own.

"The tunnel leads to the wharf," he said. "A secret route into the Tower once used by smugglers, but now long-forgotten. That is where the *Hohenzollern* is waiting – in the shadows of St Katharine Docks. We don't have much time if we are to free the King before the Kaiser sends him into exile."

Heeding his warning, Penelope turned towards the cage. She could see the King and his family tentatively approaching Monty's prone form, the dark-haired figure of Princess Victoria already kneeling solicitously by his side. The King glanced up at the sound of Penny's and Amsel's approaching footsteps.

"What fresh trickery is this?" he demanded, the Queen clutching his hand at the sight of their glowing green faces.

"Have no fear, Your Majesty," Penelope replied, the train of her velvet evening gown trailing in her wake. Fixing her mind on the iron bars impeding her path, she reached out her hands as Amsel had shown her. The King watched on aghast as Penelope's body melted through the cage as if it was made of mist. "We have come to free you from this prison."

XXII

As Princess Victoria tended to Monty's comatose form, Penelope knelt by her side. The young princess glanced up, her porcelain features betraying a flicker of fear at the pale-green sheen that marked Penny's skin.

"There is no need to worry, Your Highness," Penelope reassured her. "I am a woman just like you. I only wish to see that my Uncle Montgomery is unharmed."

With an uncertain smile, the Princess retreated to the safety of her father's side. King Edward looked on astounded as Amsel slipped through the bars of the cage as well. Penny turned her attention to Monty, still lying prone where the Kaiser's guards had left him. The rise and fall of his chest told her he was still alive, but the actor's beard was now streaked with silver and the trauma of his experience at the hands of the radiant boys was written across his face. As Penelope stared down at her fictional uncle, the actor's eyes flickered open, blinking owlishly, before he let out a cry of horror.

"What new nightmare is this?" Monty dragged himself up into a sitting position, staring back at Penny with an anguished gaze. "My God, girl, what have they done to you?"

"It is Professor Röntgen's machine," she replied, keeping her voice calm even as the pale fire raced through her veins. "It has transformed me into one of his glowing ghosts – for the moment, at least."

She reached out a hand to help Monty to his feet, but the actor backed away from her touch.

"I do not need your assistance, Penelope," he said, pulling himself to his feet. "Only a way out of this nightmare you have penned! Where on earth are we anyway?"

Monty glanced around his surroundings and then gasped as he saw King Edward glaring back at him.

"Your Majesty," Monty stuttered, bowing his head at the sight of the royal family huddled together in this dripping dungeon. "Thank the Lord, you are unharmed!"

"Can you explain what is happening here?" the King snapped, gesturing angrily towards Amsel and Penelope. "When these ghosts came to take my family, smothering us in our beds with sedative-soaked handkerchiefs that sent us into a stupor, I thought I was trapped in a dream of one of your stories, Mr Flinch. But then when we awoke in this godforsaken place, I could see that this plot was no fantasy."

"I can assure you, Your Majesty, I am innocent of all accusations that have been made. None of this is my doing—"

Penny stepped forward, cutting short Monty's grovelling reply.

"There is no time for explanations, Your Majesty. We have to get you to safety before the Kaiser's men return."

"They are already here," the King replied darkly, the sight of Amsel's naval uniform bringing a bitter frown to his brow.

Penelope shook her head. "You are mistaken, Your Majesty. It is only thanks to Sea Cadet Amsel's brave assistance that we managed to find you here at all, and it is with his aid that we will help you to escape." She turned towards the young sailor. "How do we get them out of here?"

Amsel's gaze flicked from the King to his family: Queen Alexandra, Princess Victoria, the Dukes of Connaught and York; brothers, sisters, children and grandchildren, ranging in age from babes in arms to the stout figure of Edward himself. He turned back to Penelope.

"It is impossible – the only way out is through the tunnel that leads to the wharf. The Kaiser's guards will be returning at any moment. There is no way we will be able to sneak the King and his family past them."

Penelope frowned. There had to be a way to save the King and foil the Kaiser's scheme; the alternative was too dreadful to contemplate. She reached up to brush a stray curl of hair from her forehead, her fingers still gleaming with a pale-green fire. At the sight of these, a sudden spark of inspiration shone in Penny's eyes.

"We can get them out the same way we came in," she said, gesturing towards the dripping stone walls of the cell. "Through the walls of the Tower itself."

The young sailor shook his head, dark shadows clouding his brow.

"There are too many of them, Miss Tredwell. I told you, the only way to share this curse that is pulsing through our veins is by touch alone. I could take one, possibly two with me, holding their hands as we plunge through solid stone, but even between us, there is no way we could rescue them all."

In the distance, a faint echo of footsteps could be heard; the sound of the radiant boys returning. Penelope despaired, her only hope of saving Great Britain from the Kaiser's bloodless invasion evaporating as the footsteps drew nearer. They only had minutes left. She looked back at the royal family: Princess Victoria clutching her father's hand, whilst the Queen gathered her children and grandchildren close to her, hoping in some way to forestall the inevitable. Standing close to the King, Monty fixed Penny with a desperate look, his hooded eyes filled with fear.

"You have a plan, Penelope?" he asked plaintively. "You always have a plan."

Penelope looked from the King to Monty, the two men anxiously awaiting her reply. She was struck for the first time at how alike they looked, not in garb, where the King's dress uniform put the cut of Monty's tailcoat to shame, but in bearing and countenance. The same silvered beard, the same bristling eyebrows, broad shoulders set in a stance that mirrored the other man's exactly, although the King's frame seemed a little fuller round the waist. And where the King's features were set in a look of fierce defiance, Monty's face wore a dark, haunted frown. With a sudden leap of imagination, Penny knew how they could rescue the King.

"There's only one way we can get you to safety, Your Majesty," she said. "You have to swap places with Montgomery Flinch."

XXIII

The two men stared at her astounded.

"What do you mean?" the King demanded. "How on earth will my changing places with Mr Flinch help us all to escape from this ghastly place?"

"Not all, I'm afraid," Penelope replied. "Just you, Your Majesty. You have seen how we have walked through the bars of your cage unharmed. If you take Sea Cadet Amsel's hand, he will be able to guide you safely from this place – you will even be able to walk through the walls of the Tower without any harm." She turned towards the young sailor. "You must escort the King to 10 Downing Street and inform the Prime Minister of the Kaiser's plan without delay."

Casting a nervous glance at Amsel's glowing visage, King Edward shook his head. "I do not deny the unearthly powers that you both possess, but I refuse to leave my family behind."

"But, Your Majesty," Penny protested. "The

fate of the British Empire rests on your safety. You are the bond that unites this great nation and it is to your name that they will rally. The British people hold you in the highest regard – you only have to see the coronation decorations that fill the streets to understand this. You cannot abandon them to the Kaiser's iron rule."

The King glowered from behind his silvered beard, his eyes darkening as he took in the full meaning of her words. Beneath his furrowed brow, Penny could see the struggle playing out across his features, torn between his duty to his family and the Empire at large.

Queen Alexandra rested a hand on her husband's arm, turning his face towards hers as she met his gaze with a brave smile.

"She is right, Bertie," she said, her words soft but firm. "Your country needs you more than we do now. It is your duty as their King to escape from this place unharmed."

The King clasped her hand, a solitary tear creeping from his eye.

"My dear Alix," he said. "What a remarkable woman you are. Take care of the children, my dear, and be reassured that I will return for you before that fool of a nephew of mine has even sailed past the London Docks."

"Your Majesty," said Penny, mindful that the sound of footsteps were almost upon them. "You must hurry."

With a swift nod, the King began to disrobe, unbuttoning his military greatcoat before lifting his cap to reveal his balding crown. Mute with fear, Monty began to do the same, slipping his tailcoat from his shoulders before exchanging clothes with the King.

As Penelope helped him into the King's uniform, his broad chest now shining with medals, Monty turned to her with a hiss.

"This will never work," he protested. "There is no way on God's earth that I will be able to convince the Kaiser that I'm his uncle."

"You won't have to," Penny replied. "You only have to convince his guards." Leaving Monty's side, she gathered together several of the blankets that had been discarded on the stone floor. Fashioning these into the form of a sleeping figure, she placed this mannequin in the furthest corner of the cage. "We just need to buy enough time to get the King safely away."

"But what about you?" Monty asked, casting a nervous glance into the darkness as the heavy tread of footsteps drew nearer still. "Surely these Germans can count?"

Penelope clasped her hand to her forehead, the flaw in her daring plan suddenly clear to her too. She had been so concerned with how to get the King to safety that she hadn't given any thought as to how her own presence could be hidden. There was no way she could leave Monty to face the Kaiser's men alone. The chances of him inadvertently giving the game away were far too great. But before she could answer Monty's question, another voice piped up in reply.

"You can swap places with me, Miss Tredwell."

Penelope turned to see Princess Victoria holding out her ermine robe.

"I know that I am somewhat older than you," the Princess continued. "But we share the same hairstyle and our figures are of a similar frame. Your evening gown even appears to be cut from the same cloth as mine, whilst my robe and gloves will allow you to disguise this strange glow that afflicts your complexion."

With a look of alarm, the King stepped forward in protest.

"Toria, I forbid you to accompany me. The danger is too great."

Setting her face in a stubborn line, the Princess shook her head in reply.

"It is no more dangerous than being dragged to Prussia against my will by my crazed cousin. I want to be with you, Father – I will not leave your side."

From the darkness of the tunnel, the faint glow of lantern light could now be seen: the radiant boys returning for their royal cargo. Slipping the gloves on, Penny wrapped the Princess's robe around her shoulders, drawing up its fur trim to mask the fading gleam of her features.

"Your Majesty," she pressed. "There is no time for you to argue now."

With a reluctant nod, the King acquiesced, taking his daughter's hand in his own as he stepped forward to address Amsel.

"You have the fate of nations in your hands, my boy. I trust that you will steer the right course."

With a nervous bow, the young sailor extended his hands towards the King and his daughter.

"I will do my best, Your Majesty. I only ask that you both concentrate your minds and keep hold of my hand at all times. It is the only way I can ensure your safety as we walk through the walls of the Tower."

King Edward paled, but as his daughter reached out for Amsel's hand he did the same, a muttered prayer escaping from his lips as a shimmering green glow enveloped them both.

"The Lord is my shepherd. Even though I walk through the valley of the shadow of death, I will fear no evil..."

With a final nod of farewell, Amsel stepped forward, the King and his daughter matching his step as they walked towards the stone wall of the cell. As Monty and the rest of the royal family looked on dumbfounded, Penelope held her breath, knowing all too well the sensations that would now be coursing through their veins. She watched as their shimmering figures melted into stone, disappearing into the darkness until not even their shadows remained. With a choking sob, the Queen buried her face in her handkerchief.

From the far side of the catacombs, the yellow glow of a lantern hove into view; the dark figures of the Kaiser's cadets returning to escort them into exile. Penelope glanced across at Monty, the actor now dressed in the King's uniform. Beneath the peak of his Field Marshal's cap, Monty's silvered beard and heavy-lidded gaze carried an eerie echo of the King's own countenance. Feeling Penny's gaze upon him, he turned towards her, his eyes wide with fear as the radiant boys drew near.

"They will find us out for sure," he hissed.

"Remember who you are," she replied in a hurried whisper. "Monty Maples – actor extraordinaire. It is time for you to give a royal command performance like no other. The fate of the British Empire rests on your success."

XXIV

In the shadows outside the Society for the Advancement of Science, Alfie sheltered beneath the recessed porch. He had already tried the door of the tradesmen's entrance only to discover that it was locked, and from the darkened basement windows it didn't look as though anyone would answer any knock. From the street above he could hear the sound of hansom cabs drawing up outside the German embassy next door, the chatter of voices filling the night air as the distinguished guests departed from whatever reception had been thrown there.

Through the gaps in the railings, Alfie could see the swishing hems of evening gowns, well-dressed ladies affording a glimpse of ankle as they were escorted to their waiting carriages. But Alfie's thoughts were only for Penelope. Since she had been driven away by Inspector Drake earlier that day, he hadn't heard a word. On his return, Mr Wigram had made frantic calls to New Scotland

Yard, demanding to see his ward, but every one of these requests had been rebuffed. For all they knew, Penny was now languishing in a cell next to Monty.

Before he had left, Inspector Drake had told Alfie that he was under house arrest, warning him not to leave the offices of *The Penny Dreadful*. But this was one order he refused to follow. With Penny indisposed, it was up to him now to uncover the truth of the radiant boys. It was the only way left to clear Monty's name and free Penelope. If he failed then it would be the end of *The Penny Dreadful* and he could not allow himself to imagine that.

From what Penny had told him, the answer to this mystery lay in Professor Röntgen's laboratory, hidden in this building somewhere. But how on earth was he going to get inside to find it?

As if in answer to this unspoken question, a light appeared at one of the basement windows, betraying the fact that someone was still there at this late hour. Alfie shivered, remembering the masked figures of the radiant boys. If they found him skulking here, he dreaded to think what they would do. He cast a nervous glance at the black-painted door he had seen them slip through two nights before. The sign fixed there still proclaimed: "No hawkers or pedlars. All deliveries must be made between the hours of 8.00 a.m. and 6.00 p.m."

At the sight of this, an idea sprang into Alfie's mind. If he had a reason to be here, then perhaps he could wangle his way inside. Glancing around, he grabbed hold of an empty packing crate and, rifling through the dustbins, he began to fill this with an array of discarded scientific equipment: empty bottles and beakers, broken microscopes and cracked test tubes. Fixing a discarded lid to the top of the crate, Alfie hefted this up under his arm and, turning back towards the door, reached up with his free hand to ring the bell.

In reply, a faint tinkling sound came from within, followed by the sound of footsteps shuffling towards the door. Alfie's stomach knotted in anticipation as a key rattled in the lock. Then the door was pushed open a crack, the light from inside spilling out into the shadows as a face peered around the frame.

It was an elderly man, his features disguised by the snow-white beard that consumed half of his face. For a moment, Alfie thought that this was Professor Röntgen himself, remembering Penny's description of the German scientist's prodigious beard, but as the man at the door spoke, the soft Scottish burr of his accent told Alfie that this wasn't the case.

"What do you want?" the man asked, peering at him suspiciously through the thick lenses of his spectacles.

"I have a delivery, sir."

Seeing the crate in Alfie's arms, the man shook his head reproachfully.

"No, no, no," he replied. "Ach, can't you read the sign? Strictly no deliveries after six in the evening. The Society is closed – the only reason that I am still here is to attend to my paperwork."

Alfie stood his ground. "This is an urgent delivery of scientific equipment for the attention of Professor Röntgen himself. I was instructed to bring it here without delay."

For a second, the elderly scientist seemed poised to shake his head again, but then a flicker of unease passed across his face. With a sigh, he pushed the door open, gesturing for Alfie to place the crate inside.

"What strange contraptions has he ordered now?" he murmured, motioning towards a space just inside the doorway. "Set it down there, lad, and I'll see that Professor Röntgen gets it first thing in the morning."

Keeping a tight grip on the crate, Alfie shook his head. "I'm afraid I cannot do that, sir. My guvnor said that Professor Röntgen left strict instructions that this package was to be delivered directly to his laboratory. He says that these are scientific instruments of an extremely delicate nature and I wasn't just to leave them with any Tom, Dick or Harry. No offence, sir."

Bristling at Alfie's comment, the elderly scientist scratched furiously at his beard.

"I will have you know, my boy, that I am Dr John Hughlings Jackson and I am well used to handling all manner of laboratory equipment. Professor Röntgen is attending a reception at the German embassy this evening, and will not return before tomorrow." He looked as though he was ready to slam the door in Alfie's face, but then paused for a second, a flicker of doubt flashing behind his spectacles as he remembered the disaster that had struck the last time he hadn't followed Röntgen's instructions to the letter. With an exasperated shake of his head, he beckoned Alfie inside.

"Follow me then," he sighed. "What with my conference papers to write and delivery boys turning up at all hours of the night, it does not seem as though I will get any sleep tonight."

The elderly scientist led Alfie along a broad hallway. As he hefted the crate in front of him, Alfie glanced around his surroundings, his heart thumping in his chest. The wide hall was dimly lit by electric bulbs, a low buzzing sound following their footsteps as they reached a gloomy stairwell.

"This way, this way," Dr Jackson wheezed as he led the way down a single flight of stairs. Reaching the bottom of the stairwell, another long corridor stretched out in front of them. "I really do not know why Professor Röntgen insists on hiding away down here."

Still muttering his complaints about the

German scientist's secrecy, Dr Jackson escorted Alfie to a steel door that stood at the end of the corridor. An electric lantern glowed green next to the door, casting a sickly light on the scene. Reaching down to the loop of keys on his belt, Dr Jackson unlocked the door.

"This is Professor Röntgen's laboratory. Now, if you could leave this delivery of yours, I will be able to return to my own pressing work."

The scientist flicked a light switch and, as it illuminated the room, Alfie stepped into the laboratory, the butterflies in his stomach taking flight as he stared at his surroundings. The stories he had read had led him to expect a laboratory like Dr Frankenstein's, filled with bubbling beakers and test tubes, but instead this pristine space was almost empty – just two rows of chairs in the centre of the room set facing a tall lead-lined box. Wires ran between the chairs to the ceiling and, raising his eyes, Alfie gasped as he saw the strange arrangement of glass tubes and coils that were fixed there.

"What does all this do?" he asked, gazing up in wonder at the array of machinery, more remarkable than anything he had glimpsed in the tales of scientific romance published in the pages of *The Penny Dreadful*'s competitors.

Dr Jackson stepped forward into the laboratory, peering up at the scientific equipment with a similar look of enquiry.

"I must admit that I could not tell you," he confessed. "Professor Röntgen has consulted with me extensively on my own research into matters of the human brain, but my knowledge of his research is somewhat limited." He stared intently at the glass tubes thronging the ceiling. "He has only told me that he hopes his invention will bring peace to the world."

Before Alfie could ask him about the radiant boys, the sound of a German oath turned their attention to the door.

"Another spy in our midst!" Professor Röntgen shrieked, the expression on his face as wild as his hair as he stormed into his laboratory. Seizing hold of Alfie's shoulder, he twisted him round, the wooden crate Alfie was holding clattering to the ground and spilling its contents over the floor. "What are you doing here?"

Speechless with shock, Alfie stared up at Röntgen's angry countenance, flecks of spittle speckling the scientist's beard. Dr Jackson spoke up on his behalf.

"Please calm yourself, professor. He is just a delivery boy with yet another crate of equipment for your experiments."

Loosening his grip, Professor Röntgen stared down at the scientific instruments now scattered across the floor: rusting microscopes, punctured vacuum pumps, broken bottles and beakers. Reaching down, he seized hold of a cracked slide rule, its brass gauge bent beyond all usefulness.

"What kind of experiment do you think I could conduct with this detritus?" he roared. "The boy is a spy – just like that confounded author – and he must be punished alike."

Alfie didn't have time to react as Röntgen rounded on him, lifting the heavy slide rule like a truncheon and then bringing it down on his head with a crack. The last thing he glimpsed as he slid to the floor unconscious was Dr Jackson, his face frozen in an expression of horror.

XXV

"You cannot do this, Professor Röntgen. To experiment on an individual without their express permission goes against every tenet of scientific method. It is barbarous and I will not be party to such an act."

"You said you wanted to see the discoveries that I have made, Dr Jackson. Well, here is your chance. And as for the boy, I assure you he will be unharmed."

The voices sounded as if they were coming from a tunnel, a distant echo to the words as Alfie's eyes slowly flickered open. He was slumped in a seated position, a jagged ache throbbing across his temple where Röntgen's blow had landed. Lifting his head with a grimace, Alfie saw the array of glass tubes and coils suspended above him. The realisation of where he was slowly dawned through the fog of pain. Panicking, Alfie tried to move, but then quickly realised that his arms were strapped to the seat, heavy restraints holding him in place even as he strained against them.

From behind him in the laboratory, he heard the sound of Professor Röntgen's Germanic tones.

"Besides, Dr Jackson," the professor continued, "your sudden attack of conscience would be admirable if it was not for the fact that your work has helped me to realise the full potential of this invention of mine."

"What do you mean?" Dr Jackson asked.

"Reading your research into how the brain's electrical impulses control conscious movement led to a breakthrough in my experiments to control these rays that take my name. The power of conscious thought is the secret to their mastery. The Kaiser was most pleased when I recruited you to work for the Society."

"The Kaiser? What do you mean?" Dr Jackson sounded dumbfounded. "I thought that our work here was for the common good, free from any national interest."

"Who do you think funds the Society for the Advancement of Science?" Röntgen sneered in reply. "Did you think that our location next to the Imperial German Embassy was a happy accident? The Kaiser has paid for every pipette and Bunsen burner in this building and I owe him my absolute loyalty. It was whilst working at the Kaiser's institute that I made my first discovery, and when I showed the Kaiser the fruits of my research he immediately saw their military potential: a vision of a New Atomic Army transformed by my Röntgen rays."

"But you said that your invention would bring peace to the world..."

"And so it will, Dr Jackson. The Kaiser assures me his New Atomic Army will spread peace across the globe – from the barrel of a gun, if that is what it takes. Now, let me show you the true wonder of my invention." The professor lowered his voice to a mutter as he turned towards the lead-lined chamber. "I think it is time to increase the voltage again – perhaps this will reveal at last the true limits of the human body's capacity to endure the rays' power."

His soft words sent a shiver down Alfie's spine as he sat trapped beneath Röntgen's strange machine. This must be how the German scientist had created the ghosts they had seen, and now he planned to transform Alfie into one of these radiant boys. He struggled to free himself again, but the leather restraints around his arms held firm.

"I would advise you to join me inside the control room, Dr Jackson." Professor Röntgen's voice rang across the laboratory. "It would not be wise for you to accidentally stray into the path of the rays."

Still protesting as he followed his fellow

scientist's advice, Dr Jackson disappeared into the antechamber, its lead-lined door slamming shut behind them both. There was a moment of silence and then Alfie heard the beginning whine of an electrical generator. Twisting his head, he saw the wires running from the lead-lined box, encased in insulating India rubber. These wires cut a route through the centre of the room, skirting the place where Alfie was seated before leading along the wall and ceiling to connect to the strange array of glass tubes suspended above his head. The humming noise grew louder followed by an answering crackle from the copper coils curled inside the tubes. A faint green glow began to radiate from the apparatus, the same light Alfie had seen in the faces of the radiant boys.

With a mounting sense of terror, Alfie glanced around wildly, desperately looking for a way to free himself. The leather straps holding his arms in place were pulled tight, but the restraints around his legs hung loose. In front of him he could see the rubber-insulated cables running along the floor to the ceiling; the crackle of electricity in the coils above his head told him that he didn't have much time left. Scattered across the floor were the contents of the crate with which he'd bluffed his way into this place: broken scientific instruments, shattered beakers and cracked test tubes. The nearest of these lay tantalisingly close: a glass vial resting on top of the rubber cables.

Alfie realised that there was only one way he could stop Röntgen's machine before it turned him into a living ghost. The only risk was that it would kill him in the process. He glanced up again at the suspended glass tubes slowly glowing with a flickering green light and shuddered. It was worth the risk.

Stretching out his leg, Alfie tried to reach the test tube, his hobnailed boot nudging the glass vial as green shadows danced across his face and the whine of the machinery reached a crescendo. Grinding his heel, he crushed the test tube beneath his foot, the splintering glass cutting through the insulating rubber to expose the wires beneath. His head spinning with the effort, he stamped his boot down again, the iron nails on his sole meeting the wire with a thunderous crack, sending a shower of sparks into the air.

The laboratory was plunged into darkness, the short circuit he'd created cutting the power completely. Alfie shook his head in disbelief. He had done it; the rubber sole on his hobnailed boot saving him from certain electrocution. But his sense of relief curdled as he looked up to see the flames quickly spreading across the laboratory. The heat from the overloaded wire had ignited the insulation, the blaze following the cables to the apparatus above his head. Alfie heard it creak as he struggled against the restraints that still held him. Instead of electrocution, it looked as though he would be burned or crushed to death instead.

From behind him he heard the sound of the door to the antechamber crash open.

"What has happened here?" Professor Röntgen roared. "My invention – it must be saved!"

Alfie felt hands reaching for him in the gloom. In the light cast by the flickering flames, he glimpsed Dr Jackson's face, the elderly scientist struggling to unfasten the straps that held him prisoner.

"Quickly, lad," the scientist hissed. "We must get out of this place. The man has gone mad."

As the restraints were loosened, Alfie struggled to his feet. Taking Dr Jackson's arm in his own he blundered through the shadows in search of the door. Thick black smoke was filling the laboratory, and the two of them spluttered for breath. Alfie scrabbled to find the door handle, swinging the steel door open to bring them some respite. Pushing Dr Jackson out in front of him, Alfie glanced back to see Professor Röntgen desperately trying to smother the flames, but the fire was already consuming his invention, the array of peculiarly-shaped tubes shattering in a shower of glass. Leaving Röntgen behind to his fate, they fled the darkened building, stumbling through the blackness until they reached the street above.

Looking down through the railings, Alfie could

see the basement windows of the Society lit with a pale-orange glow. Dr Jackson turned towards him, the scientist's face blanched as white as his beard.

"We must telephone the Metropolitan Fire Brigade. My life's work lies within that building. It cannot be sacrificed to this conflagration that Professor Röntgen's mania has brought upon us."

Alfie nodded his head as the street lights along Carlton House Terrace flickered in reply. "And Inspector Drake of the Metropolitan Police Service as well," he said. "I think he will have some questions to ask about exactly what Professor Röntgen has been doing here."

He glanced down again at the basement windows, the orange glow growing brighter now. Alfie could only hope that there would be enough evidence left to exonerate Monty and Penelope.

XXVI

The Kaiser's men threw open the door of the cage, the jaundiced glow of their lanterns illuminating their glowing green skin. The radiant boys' dark disguises had now been discarded for the uniforms of the Imperial German Navy, and as the leading figure stepped into the cell, the freshly stitched gold stripe on his sleeve showed his recent promotion to the rank of midshipman.

"If you and your family would be kind enough to accompany us, Your Majesty, we will escort you to your quarters aboard the *Hohenzollern*. The Kaiser has made every preparation to ensure that you will have a comfortable voyage."

Standing in the shadows, Monty hesitated, the fear of discovery flashing across his eyes as the midshipman awaited his reply.

There was a moment of silence, then Queen Alexandra stepped forward, taking Monty's arm in her own.

"Come now, Bertie," she said with a slight tremor in her voice. "We do not wish to keep your nephew waiting."

With a stiff nod of agreement, Monty led the Queen out of the cell, the lantern light picking out the sheen of the medals pinned to his chest. As the rest of the royal family trooped out behind him, the young princes and princesses carried by their mothers, the midshipman cast a glance back into the shadows of the cell where a slumped shape could just be glimpsed beneath a blanket.

"Sleep well, Mr Flinch," he said, locking the cage door with a clang.

Ahead of him, Monty shivered as the Queen clung to his arm. The radiant boys marched in step with the royal party, no chance of escape from their escort. The gleam of their lanterns illuminated the tunnel as it slowly twisted upwards, the passageway hewn from the dripping black rock, hundreds of years before. They walked in silence, the muffled cries of Prince Henry lying swaddled in the Duchess of York's arms the only sound that could be heard, apart from the tread of their footsteps.

In the midst of the royal party, Penelope was hidden between the towering figures of the Dukes of Connaught and York. As the slope of the tunnel began to incline, she could hear the creaking of ships, shifting in their sleep, and in place of the stale subterranean air she felt the first whispers of a breeze on her face. They were nearing the river now.

The midshipman's voice echoed from the rear.

"You must board the *Hohenzollern* without delay. Do not attempt to flee, Your Majesty, unless you wish to find yourself taking residence at the bottom of the Thames."

The mocking laughter of the radiant boys followed Monty's shaking footsteps as they emerged into the night. Stepping out of the tunnel behind him, Penny risked a glance up at the sky. Dark clouds were scudding across the moon, its broken beams playing upon a narrow pathway of grey, glittering water, whilst on either side of this, the river was black with dozens of hulls, their funnels and masts as thick as a forest. But amidst these ships, one vessel stood resplendent, her gleaming gold and white paintwork stretching along the quayside, twin smokestacks the colour of burnished brass silhouetted against the sky. The pride of the Imperial German Navy: His Majesty's Yacht *Hohenzollern*.

Beyond this, Penny's gaze traced the shape of the Tower wharves, the distant figures of red-coated sentries patrolling their gravelled walks. Too far away, she saw with a scowl, for any chance of rescue from that quarter. The Tower's turrets and battlements peered out over the water and Penelope prayed that Amsel had been able to guide the King and Princess Victoria safely through its walls.

The Kaiser's marines hurried them towards the ship's gangway and, with Queen Alexandra still clinging tightly to his arm, Monty began to ascend the steps.

As they boarded the ship, Penelope held the fur trim of her robe across her face, seemingly to protect herself from the chill of the night air, but in reality hiding the pale-green glow that still shone from her features. From the quayside she heard the rattle of a heavy chain suddenly let go, followed by the clicking of the capstan-pails as the ship heaved anchor. The deck was alive with scurrying sailors, but at the sight of the glowing figures of the Kaiser's guards the sailors backed away superstitiously and the radiant boys escorted the royal retinue below decks without a word.

As the ship rolled in the swell, Penny reached out a gloved hand to steady herself, but found her fingers grasping empty air. Stumbling forward, she almost fell into Monty as he reached the bottom step, the fur trim of her robe falling from her face for a second. As the actor turned in alarm, panic in his gaze as he glimpsed her glowing features, the sound of a German voice rang out from the corridor.

"What are you doing?"

The midshipman stepped forward, wary of any attempt to escape. As Monty's bulky frame shielded her from his view, Penny pulled up the fur trim to mask her face again.

"I'm terribly sorry," she replied. "I'm afraid that I haven't quite got my sea legs yet."

With a snort of amusement, the bumptious midshipman turned back to lead them along the corridor.

"Do not worry, Your Royal Highness," he called back over his shoulder. "You'll have plenty of time to find them on the voyage home."

The broad corridor was carpeted in a thick silver-grey pile, whilst maple doors adorned with ivory handles branched off to the left and to the right. If it wasn't for the rolling motion beneath her feet as the ship got under steam, Penelope would have sworn that she was walking through the hall of some grand manor house instead.

"These are the guest suites," the midshipman continued. "Each cabin has been prepared with everything that you will require."

With typical Teutonic efficiency, the guards escorted each branch of the royal family tree to their own stateroom: the Duke and Duchess of York with the young princes and princess; the Duke of Connaught; Princess Louise; Prince Alfred; and the Duke of Albany – every single person ahead of Kaiser Wilhelm in the British line of succession now imprisoned in the gilded cage of his royal yacht. And outside every door, the radiant boys stood guard in silence. No chance of escape beneath their gleaming gazes.

The midshipman flung open the door to the final stateroom. With a respectful nod he gestured for the last of the radiant boys to usher Queen Alexandra, Monty and Penelope inside.

"I do hope the accommodation is to your satisfaction, Your Majesty. I am sure you will find it more comfortable than your recent room at the Tower."

Monty stifled a gasp as he entered the stateroom. Luxurious armchairs and sofas were arranged on a magnificent Persian rug, whilst a burnished mahogany table was laid with military precision. Between the floral decorations and candelabras, Penny could see a sumptuous feast: plates laden with cooked meats, silver tureens of vegetables and breads of every description. The grand stateroom was decorated with fabrics and furnishings of the most ostentatious design, whilst paintings of famous naval victories hung from the walls.

"The voyage to Prussia should not take very long," the midshipman informed them from the doorway. "The Kaiser sends his apologies that he could not welcome you aboard in person, but he is currently at the ship's helm as the *Hohenzollern* navigates the Thames. The fog is rising and this waterway can be a treacherous one for a ship of this size. Once we reach the North Sea, however, he will join you to discuss the matter of his coronation."

With a clipped nod of his head, the midshipman closed the cabin door behind him, the click of a key in the lock reminding them all that this floating palace was their prison. As Penny's gaze roved around the cabin, searching fruitlessly for an escape route, Monty strode towards the banquet table. He reached for a crystal decanter that was filled with a dark-burgundy liquid and with a trembling hand poured a generous measure into an empty goblet. Taking a heavy gulp from the glass, Monty flopped down onto the nearest sofa.

"We may as well make ourselves comfortable while we await our discovery," he declared. "Perhaps once Kaiser Bill realises that the King hasn't actually joined him on this pleasure cruise, he will return us safely to port."

Penny stared back at Monty, unable to believe his optimism as she watched him take another gulp from his glass. She remembered the cruel gleam in the Kaiser's eyes as he consigned Monty to the Tower. Somehow she didn't think he would react so calmly to finding him here in the royal guest suite. But before she had the chance to voice her concerns, the sound of a sob turned Penny's gaze towards Queen Alexandra.

Now perched on an armchair facing Monty, the Queen fixed him with a plaintive stare.

"You do think they have made it out of that place, don't you, Mr Flinch?" she asked, gulping out the words between hiccuping sobs. "The shame of exile will be hard enough to bear, but I could not countenance the thought of losing dear Bertie and darling Toria too." As this final sentence escaped her lips, the Queen's features crumpled as she wept fresh tears of imagined grief.

With panic in his eyes, Monty turned to Penelope in search of support. Casting all questions of etiquette to one side, Penny knelt in front of the Queen, reaching inside her own pocket to extricate her handkerchief before proffering this to Her Majesty. Delicately plucking it from Penelope's phosphorescent fingers, the Queen blew her nose with a tremulous honk.

"You are so kind, my dear," she sniffed. "And brave, too, for one so young. I imagine you have inherited your valour from your uncle." Folding her hands to restore her composure, Queen Alexandra lifted her gaze to Monty again. "I fear you will need every ounce of your bravery, Mr Flinch, when Wilhelm discovers your deception. My nephew is a callous and capricious man, and when he finds out that his Uncle Bertie has escaped to reclaim his throne, I dread to think what his reaction will be to the man who has taken his place. We are heading for the open sea and Wilhelm will not feel bound by the laws of the land, or indeed any notions of common decency and fair play. I shudder to think what he is capable of."

Behind his beard, Monty paled, his ashen complexion a striking contrast to the fading glow that still marked Penelope's skin.

Below them in the depths of the ship, Penny could feel the throb of the engines as they slowly picked up speed, the royal yacht navigating her passage around the river's curves as she steamed east with the tide. Her mind raced at the same quickening rate, desperate to find a way out of this perilous situation they found themselves in: imprisoned, their discovery imminent and no prospect of rescue as the radiant boys stood guard outside the cabin door. She didn't even know if the King had escaped from the Tower alive, let alone made it to 10 Downing Street to raise the alarm.

A sudden resolve stole over Penelope. "Do not worry, Your Majesty," she said. "We will not stay here to await the Kaiser's displeasure. My uncle and I will find some other way of raising the alarm before the *Hohenzollern* leaves London. The Kaiser must not have the opportunity to use your captivity as any kind of bargaining chip to wrest the Crown from the King."

Queen Alexandra stared up at her open-mouthed, astounded by Penny's clear thinking and resolute spirit.

"You have divined my very fears, dear girl, although I was loath to speak them. I worry that there are no depths to which Wilhelm will not stoop to realise his hateful scheme – even to the extent of harming his own flesh and blood."

Monty was also staring at Penny, but with an uneasy look in his eye.

"But how are we supposed to raise the alarm?" he asked, gesturing towards the stateroom door. "There are guards stationed outside whose very touch would turn us into ghosts just like them." The actor shook his head in resignation as he drained his goblet.

In answer to his question, Penny strode towards Monty. Concentrating her mind, she took the glass from his hand and set it on the table beside him.

"What are you doing?" he blustered.

Penelope took hold of his hand, Monty moaning in fear as her luminous fingers meshed with his own; flesh and bone melting together as Röntgen's rays transformed them both.

"What is happening to me?" the actor breathed as a shimmering glow crept across his skin. He struggled to free himself from her grasping hand. "Please, Penelope – this time you ask too much of me. Spare me this, please."

"I need your help," Penny replied, refusing to relinquish her grip. "I cannot do this alone. We have to raise the alarm before the Kaiser discovers us here. For King and country, Monty, will you help me, please?"

Behind his agitated gaze, something stirred in Monty's eyes: a faint spark of patriotism shining through a cloud of red wine and cowardice. After what seemed like an age, he finally gave her his reply.

"What do you want me to do?"

XXVII

"Help me, please!" Queen Alexandra rapped sharply on the cabin door. "My husband is feeling quite unwell."

In reply, the heavy door remained locked, but as a luminous face emerged from the other side, the Queen quickly drew back in fear. The guard's glowing green gaze peered through the wood as if it were merely water. The sailor saw Monty lying slumped against the mahogany table, his head resting insensibly on his chest whilst a burgundy stain spread from his upturned wine glass.

"Is this another of the Kaiser's tricks?" the Queen demanded as the radiant boy slipped into the room. "Not only to steal my husband's throne, but to poison him as well?"

With a look of alarm, the sailor hurried towards the unconscious figure he believed to be the King, not noticing Penelope as she emerged from the shadows behind him. As he lifted Monty's head from his chest, the young sailor let out an oath of surprise as Penny brought the crystal decanter down on his head with a crack.

"Bravo!" Monty cried out, scrambling to his feet as the sailor slumped to the floor in his place. He watched as Penny set the crystal decanter back on the table before stooping over the sailor's unconscious form. "But I do hope you didn't spill any of that wine, Penelope. It wouldn't be worth wasting a drop on that blighter."

Glancing up, Penny cast the actor a reproving glare.

"I did not wish to harm him," she said, pressing her fingers to the sailor's neck to reassure herself that he still breathed. "He is as much a pawn in this game as we are, but there was no other way to get past him without discovery."

Reaching down, Penelope lifted a ring of keys from the sailor's pocket. As Queen Alexandra watched her with a pensive frown, she rose to her feet again.

"As soon as the coast is clear, Your Majesty, you must release your family and head for the lifeboats," Penelope said, presenting the keys to the Queen. "My uncle and I will create a diversion to draw the guards from their posts. It is your only chance of escape."

Her expression grave, Queen Alexandra nodded her assent.

"But how will you divert the guards?" she asked. "There are so many of them and you are only a girl."

"I am a young lady of many resources," Penny replied, the pale lustre of her skin gleaming beneath the lamplight. "I am sure that I will be able to find a way."

She turned to face Monty, holding out her hand towards him as the actor trembled with fear.

"Are you ready?" she said.

With a gulp, Monty nodded his head, reluctantly taking hold of her hand.

"Are you sure about this, Penelope?" he said, his voice quavering as the same shimmering glow enveloped him too. "This quickening of the blood is almost more than I can bear."

"Just concentrate your mind," she replied, keeping hold of his hand as they stepped towards the door. "The fate of the British Empire depends upon it."

Before Monty had the chance to protest again, Penny plunged them both forward. She felt her mind whirl as they slipped through the door, fire racing through her veins as her body vibrated in time with the atoms around her. Before she could even make sense of these sensations, they were on the other side, Monty wheezing as they emerged into the corridor outside.

"How do you bear this?" he moaned. "I feel as though my very soul is about to explode."

Penelope hushed him, silently gesturing towards the figures of the radiant boys standing guard all along the corridor. Not one set of eyes were turned in their direction.

"This way," she hissed, keeping Monty's hand in her own. The two of them hurried towards the stairs at the corridor's end. As they crept out of sight, Monty turned towards her, a cold sweat soaking his brow.

"Where are we going?" he asked.

"To the engine room," Penelope replied. "We have to stop the ship before it leaves the Thames."

Below her, she could hear the thud-thud of the engines as the ship slowly turned, the river straightening as they steamed past the East India Docks. Keeping a tight hold of Monty's hand, Penny hurried down the stairs, the silver-grey carpet giving way to polished steel as they reached the lower deck. A long corridor stretched out in front of them. Penelope peered fearfully ahead as the clanking din of the engines beckoned her on.

"Where are the sailors?" Monty asked, glancing timorously into an empty mess room as they hurried along the corridor.

"Most will be above decks now," Penny replied. "If the fog is rising, the Kaiser will have lookouts posted at every vantage point to ensure our safe passage."

Peering past every door, she glimpsed naval stores and baggage holds, workshops and cramped compartments, every one of these rooms deserted to prove the truth of her words.

The endless rumble of engine noise was growing louder still, its ceaseless thrum reminding her of the strange vibration that still pulsed through her veins. Penny glanced down at her hand, the pale lustre of her skin seemingly starting to fade. Amsel had said that the effects of Röntgen's rays were only temporary. She could only pray that they would last for a little while longer.

The hiss of Monty's voice in her ear jolted Penny from her preoccupation.

"This is it."

Through an open doorway, she saw the pipe-packed space of the engine room, the rumble of the propeller shafts now turned to a roar. Steam rose from the maze of vibrating machinery, the continuously pumping rods throwing off a fine splatter of oil that clung to the uniforms of the two German sailors manning the huge brass wheels of the throttle station.

Monty flattened himself to the wall outside.

"What are we supposed to do?" he said, his voice barely audible above the noise. "Ask them nicely if they'll turn back round?"

Peering round the edge of the door, Penny assessed the situation. The two stocky sailors were facing away from them, their eyes fixed to the countless clocks and gauges that made sense of the engine's guttural roar. The shrill ring of a bell cut through the tumult, turning the sailors' attention towards the engine room telegraph, its brass arrow now pointing to half steam ahead. With a swab of a greasy cloth, the shorter of the two sailors turned the throttle wheel overhead, the answering thud of the piston rods telling him that the *Hohenzollern* would soon be picking up speed. Penelope bit her lip. If the river was fogbound, the Kaiser must be throwing all caution to the wind. She had to stop him somehow.

Her gaze alighted on a coal-stained shovel resting just outside the doorway, left there by some weary stoker perhaps. Turning towards Monty, she cupped her hand to his ear so he could hear her over the roar.

"We have to stop the ship."

"But the sailors..."

Penelope reached for the shovel, pushing it into Monty's protesting hands.

"All we need to do is take them unawares," she said. "A swift knock to the back of the head should put them out for the count. Then we can create the diversion we need to allow the royal family to escape."

Monty stared down at the shovel in dismay.

"But I'm an actor, not a fighter!"

Fixing Monty with a resolute stare, Penny searched for the words to give him the courage he needed.

"Every man must fight for his country," she told him. "And I'm sure King Edward will richly reward the man who almost single-handedly rescues his family and returns him to the throne."

At the prospect of this, Monty tightened his grip on the shovel.

"We'll have to be quick," he hissed. "I do not fancy my chances against those fellows in any kind of a brawl."

Penny nodded. Gesturing for Monty to lead the way, the two of them crept into the engine room, the sound of their footsteps lost in the maelstrom of noise. The two sailors were oblivious to their presence as Monty skulked behind them, their attention held rapt by the readings from the engine's gauges. But as he raised the shovel to strike the first blow, a reflection in the glass casing caused one of the sailors to turn in alarm.

"Gott im Himmel!"

As Monty struck, the sailor ducked under the blow, the blade of the shovel cracking against a brass gauge before falling to the floor with a clatter. Then the sailor was upon him, his hands reaching for Monty's throat as he grappled him towards the huge engine block.

Alerted by his crewmate, the second sailor grabbed hold of Penelope. She cried out in pain as his brutish grip crushed the bones in her wrists. Wreathed in a halo of steam, she saw his shocked gaze as he focused for the first time on her glowing green visage. Concentrating her mind, Penny felt her body vibrate in time with the atoms in his fingers as she slipped from his grasp like a ghost.

The sailor stared back at her in horror, crossing himself as he uttered a single word like a curse.

"*Lorelei!*"

Penny stooped to retrieve the shovel.

"No, it's Penelope," she replied, bringing the handle up sharply into his stomach. Then, as the winded sailor sank to his knees, she clonked the flat side of the shovel against his crown, knocking him out cold.

Her own assailant dealt with, Penny turned to see Monty pinioned against the vast engine block. With a snarl, the burly sailor tightened his grip, twisting Monty's face towards its hammering pistons. The actor's cries were lost in a tumult of steam, the hissing steel threatening to shave off more than his beard. But before the sailor could push home his advantage, a look of stunned confusion spread across his face. Releasing his grip on Monty's throat, he slowly slid to the floor. Penelope stood behind him with the shovel in her hand.

"Thank God," Monty gasped, rubbing his neck with trembling fingers. "I thought I was mincemeat."

As the actor pulled himself free, the shrill peal of the engine-room telegraph turned Penny's gaze back to the throttle deck.

"Quick," she said, stepping towards the throttle station. "We have to stop the ship." Penelope stared up at the controls: a dizzying array of gauges and dials, levers and wheels. "But how do we do it?"

Monty joined her at the control panel, still breathing hard. "Well, we could put the engines hard astern," he said, scratching his head thoughtfully. "But then we'd run the risk of the tide catching the ship and taking her sideways. I think a wiser course of action would be to turn the throttle wheel into reverse until the engines come to a halt."

Penny turned towards him in astonishment.

"How on earth do you know all this?"

A purple flush coloured Monty's features as he reached up to grasp the huge throttle wheel.

"I auditioned for the part of Captain Corcoran in a production of *HMS Pinafore* at the Lyceum back in '98. My preparations for the role were meticulous." A frown furrowed Monty's brow as he strained to turn the polished brass wheel. "And yet I was still beaten to the part by that young upstart Seymour Hicks."

With a whine its handle slowly started to turn, the rise and fall of the pistons in the maze of machinery gradually slowing to a stately waltz. Leaning hard on the wheel, Monty let out a final grunt of effort, which was answered by a terminal hiss of steam escaping from the innards of the engine as it eventually came to a halt.

For a moment, the ship creaked, the sound

unnaturally loud now that the engine had been silenced; their smooth progress now replaced by a rolling wallow as the *Hohenzollern* started to drift with the tide. Then the deafening peal of the engine-room telegraph made Monty and Penny jump.

"What do we do now?" Monty asked. The brass arrow was now pointing full steam ahead, the Kaiser not realising that his orders were falling on deaf ears.

"They will come to find out what has happened to the engine," Penny replied. "This will give the Queen and her family the diversion they need to escape to the lifeboats."

"And we will join them there too?" Monty asked with a glimmer of hope in his eyes.

Penny shook her head.

"Not yet," she said, her pale-green eyes still shining even as the sheen of her skin lost its lustre. "If the King didn't make it out of the Tower alive, then we are the only two people who can save the British Empire from the Kaiser's clutches. We have to get to the bridge and find a way to stop him for good."

XXVIII

Penelope and Monty retraced their steps through the heart of the ship, scurrying past deserted staff cabins as they climbed the decks in search of the bridge. With every moment that passed, Penny could feel herself weakening, the strange fire from Röntgen's rays threatening to consume her at last. She stumbled as she reached a final flight of stairs, the sign pointing upwards indicating that they had at last reached their goal: *Kommandobrücke* – the ship's bridge.

"Are you all right, Penelope?" Monty asked, stooping to her aid, but then the actor froze as he heard a clatter of boots from the deck above. With a trembling hand, Penny grabbed hold of Monty's arm, glancing round their surroundings in search of a hiding place. The nearest door lay directly behind them, but as she turned to try the handle she discovered it was locked. The thunder of footsteps was now descending the stairs – a dozen or more men perhaps: in another second they would be discovered.

Concentrating her mind, she pulled Monty close to her; the two of them slipped through the door like ghosts before the fire in her veins was finally extinguished. For a moment Penny stood there, her head spinning, as on the other side of the door the heavy tread of footsteps stomped past: the Kaiser's men hurrying to discover what act of sabotage had brought the ship to a standstill.

As Monty wheezed, Penny glanced around the room. They were standing in what looked like a sick bay. A row of empty cots separated by flimsy curtains filled most of the room, whilst a tall medicine cabinet was set on the facing wall. But Penelope's eyes were drawn to the mirror fixed to the wall directly in front of her, a gasp escaping from her lips as she saw her own reflection.

Apart from her usual pale-green gaze, Penny's face was drained of the luminescence that had once shone from her skin. The shining green glow was now replaced with a deathly pallor. Dark shadows lurked beneath her eyes as what felt like a deadweight hung heavy on her frame, the pained creaks of the ship as it drifted with the tide echoed by the ache in her bones.

Half turning, she pressed her hands to the door. Penelope tried to focus her mind one last time, but felt only unyielding wood beneath her fingers. Amsel had said that the effects of Röntgen's rays would pass. Now it looked as though all hope of raising the alarm was gone with them too.

"The effects of Professor Röntgen's rays have left me. We're trapped," she said, turning to Monty. "The only way we can get out of here is by breaking down this door."

Monty paled. "But if we do that then they will discover us for sure," he said, the faint echo of footsteps still within earshot outside the door. "They will probably march us right up to the bridge and deliver us into the Kaiser's hands."

At Monty's reply, a glint of inspiration sparkled in Penny's eyes.

"Then that's what we have to do," she said. "Convince them to take us to the Kaiser himself. If we can reach the bridge, then maybe we can find a way to stop him at last."

"But how—"

"You have already fooled the guards once, making them believe that you really are King Edward the Seventh. Now you have to do it again. Insist that you must speak to your nephew, the Kaiser, on a matter of the utmost importance. It is the only chance we have left – a performance to save the nation. The fate of the Empire itself rests upon your talents as an actor, Monty, and I do not think you will disappoint."

At Penelope's glowing words of praise, a new light shone in Monty's eyes. Throwing his shoulders back, he stared hard at his reflection in the mirror. Beneath the peak of a Field Marshal's cap, his silver-streaked beard lent his features the likeness of King Edward, whilst the gold buttons and braid on his dress uniform glinted royally.

Monty turned back towards Penny, his countenance set in an expression of stout determination.

"I must admit, Penelope, that I had not imagined taking my final bow in front of an audience of Kaiser Bill and his ghostly crew, but I suppose it is not for any of us to choose the manner of our leaving the stage."

Penelope looked up at Monty, a stray tear glistening in the corner of her pale-green eyes.

"This won't be your final performance, Monty," she said. "We will get out of this, I promise you."

"Come what come may," he replied with a faint twinkle of the old Monty in his gaze. "Time and the hour runs through the roughest day." With a gentle bow, the actor turned back to face the locked door. "Now, you had better step back, Penelope," he said, raising his boot as he braced himself against the doorframe. "Once more unto the breach, dear friend, once more."

Kicking out with all the force he could muster, Monty sent the door flying open with a splintering crack. Straightening the buttons on his uniform as they strained to contain his ample frame, Monty held out his hand for Penelope and the two of them stepped out into the corridor as a band of imperial sailors bore down on them.

Before any of the sailors even had the chance to speak, Monty turned towards them with a peremptory stare.

"What is the meaning of this delay?" he barked. "Has my nephew forgotten how to pilot a ship? I certainly gave him enough lessons at Cowes in his youth."

The sailors stared at him dumbfounded, the groans of the *Hohenzollern* adding weight to Monty's words as the ship drifted with the tide.

"I demand to see the Kaiser," he continued, his regal tone brooking no argument. "I must speak to him now before he imperils us all."

As the ordinary sailors exchanged anxious glances, their senior officer stepped to the fore. The single stripe on his sleeve revealed his lieutenant's rank.

"The Kaiser gave strict orders that you and your family were to be confined to your quarters for the duration of the voyage, Your Majesty." The officer raised his voice above the creaks of the becalmed ship. "May I ask what you were doing in the sick bay?"

"My daughter has been afflicted with a bout of seasickness," Monty replied brusquely. "Thanks to my nephew's bungling navigation. I was looking for a tonic to soothe her constitution, but your medical supplies seem to be sadly deficient. Now, take me to see the Kaiser without delay or do you wish to go down with the tide?"

A flicker of uncertainty passed across the lieutenant's features, but as the *Hohenzollern* let out another groan of protest, he quickly made up his mind.

"Very well, Your Majesty," he said, gesturing towards the flight of stairs in front of them. "I will escort you both to the bridge."

Behind the collar of her robe, Penelope allowed herself a faint smile. So far Monty's performance as the King had been a theatrical tour de force. Now the fate of them all rested on her finding a coup de théâtre that could bring the Kaiser's plot to an end. She crossed her fingers as they climbed the steps to the bridge. It was time to make a final stand against this silent invasion.

XXIX

The bridge lay in darkness but the frantic sound of barked commands cut through the gloom. Shadowy figures scurried between the ship's telegraphs, ringing down orders to an engine room that no longer responded. Through the windows that spanned the deck Penelope could glimpse a veil of scattering fog. Faint lights on the shoreline seemed to loom perilously close, the *Hohenzollern* listing slightly as it drifted with the tide.

She strained her eyes to make sense of the scene, the dim light cast from a compass binnacle revealing the figure of a man at the helm of the bridge. As he turned his gaze from starboard to port, Penny saw this was the Kaiser, now resplendent in the uniform of a British Admiral of the Fleet. The Emperor's face was a mask of barely suppressed fury, his right hand gripping the wheel as he struggled to keep the ship from floundering.

Behind Monty and Penelope, the nervous cough of the lieutenant drew the Kaiser's gaze in their direction.

"What are you doing here, Uncle?" he snarled, addressing the question to Monty alone. "You are meant to be confined to quarters with the rest of your inconvenient brood!"

"I – I – I thought you could do with some fresh sailing lessons," Monty began, the faltering quaver in his words betraying his nerves. "Since you seem to be incapable of navigating our safe passage on this voyage."

In the darkness of the bridge the actor's features were hidden beneath the shade of his peaked cap, but as Monty spoke, the expression on the Kaiser's face changed to one of bewildered rage. He stepped away from the ship's wheel with a snarl, the ship lurching as he lunged towards Monty.

Losing her balance, Penny was thrown forwards, crashing into the teak housing of the fore bridge. Dazed, she slumped to the floor as the Kaiser grabbed hold of Monty's throat.

"Montgomery Flinch," he roared as the shadows fell from Monty's face. "Where is my uncle? Where is the King?"

The two men clung to each other as the ship reeled towards the shore, the lookout on the foredeck shouting out an oath of warning. On the bridge, one of the sailors dived to take the helm again, pulling hard on the ship's wheel as the *Hohenzollern* skirted the Isle of Dogs.

Monty's eyes bulged as the Kaiser squeezed hard.

"How dare you!" he snarled. "This is my ship. This will soon be my country to rule over too and yet still you persist with your meddling."

Spittle flecked the Kaiser's pomaded moustache as he tightened his grip. Penny saw Monty's eyes roll back in his head, the Emperor's rage choking him to within seconds of his life. As the sailors advanced towards her, she looked up at the forest of instruments arrayed on the fore bridge controls. There were countless dials and switches, gauges and buttons, their purpose known only to the most practised of mariners. Time was running out. No chances left now to raise the alarm.

Then she saw it, a single word printed beneath a dangling lanyard: NEBELHORN – the ship's horn.

Reaching up, Penny grabbed hold of the lanyard. Pulling hard on this, the ship's horn responded with a prolonged blast. The advancing sailors covered their ears as its deafening bellow sounded across the Thames. A noise loud enough to wake the city itself: the universal signal for a ship in distress.

Releasing his grip on Monty's neck, the Kaiser strode towards Penelope. With a swipe of his right arm, he knocked her off her feet. The ship's horn finally silenced as she crashed against the bridge.

"You English are mad – mad as March hares," the Kaiser hissed, turning towards Penny with murder in his eyes. "To send a mere girl to fight for your country. Once you had splendid troops, officers and men. Where are they now?" Fixing her with a venomous glare, his hand reached for the hilt of his sword. "I only trust you will die as bravely as any soldier."

Penny stared up in horror as the Kaiser drew his rapier, the blade glinting in the moonlight. But before he could strike, a deafening chorus of ships' horns sounded in reply, their ear-splitting roars seemingly coming from every direction.

"What is this?" the Kaiser gasped. "It can't be..."

Taking advantage of his distraction, Penelope scrambled to Monty's side. The actor's face was as grey as his beard as she helped him to his knees, but as the two of them turned to look through the window of the bridge there was a glimmer of hope in his eyes. Penelope shook her head in stunned disbelief as she saw the spectacle that was causing the Kaiser's despair.

As the fog slowly cleared, they could see that the Thames was thick with a flotilla of ships. Frigates, cruisers, corvettes and countless gunboats: the pride of the Royal Navy bearing down on the *Hohenzollern* from all sides. Before the Kaiser could even give his crew the order to take arms, dozens of Royal Marines were boarding the ship from the foredeck and aft. At the sight of Britain's naval might, the German sailors lay down their weapons without protest, the Royal Marines advancing upon the bridge with a singular purpose. In the shadow of the lifeboats she saw the royal family being escorted to safety, Queen Alexandra lifting her gaze with a look of thankful relief.

As the Kaiser cursed, Penny caught sight of two unexpected figures amidst the boarding party. The portly figure of King Edward the Seventh, dressed in the uniform of the First Admiral of the Fleet, now accompanied by the more soberly dressed First Lord of the Treasury, Arthur Balfour. And behind them, his features half hidden beneath a Royal Navy cap, she glimpsed a face that caused her heart to quicken: Sea Cadet Alexander Amsel, the boy now wearing the borrowed uniform of a British sailor. Penelope flushed with relief.

Entering through both wings of the bridge, the advance guard of Royal Marines quickly disarmed the German Emperor and the rest of his officers.

"This is an act of war," the Kaiser spat, surrendering his sword with a snarl.

"How dare you!" his uncle's voice boomed in reply. King Edward marched onto the bridge, fixing his nephew with a furious glare. "You have abducted my family from their beds, held us captive in the dungeons of the Tower, attempted to force me into exile so that you can steal my throne, and yet you have the audacity to accuse me of warmongering!"

Penelope watched as the Kaiser returned his uncle's glare with a withering stare.

"You would have done well to heed my advice, Uncle Bertie," he replied coldly. "And spend the rest of your days safely in exile. You may have your grand coronation, for all the good it will do you. I will soon return to these shores, but with my New Atomic Army by my side. Britain will fall along with the rest of Europe as well, but this time I will not spare you the bloodshed."

In response to his nephew's chilling threat, the King stared at him open-mouthed, his worst fears taking flight as he pictured the prospect of war. But before he had the chance to muster his reply, Balfour's bloodless tones cut across them both.

"Your Majesty, if I might reply on your government's behalf?"

With a nod of irritation, the King acquiesced and Balfour now turned to address the Kaiser.

"Your Majesty," he began again. "Any act of provocation on the part of the German nation would be dealt with most severely. You only have to look out of the window now to remind yourself of the strength of the Royal Navy. There is no way your troops would even make it across the North Sea – the British fleet would sink every one of your ships."

Beneath his ridiculous moustache, a sly grin spread across the Kaiser's face.

"Britannia may have ruled the waves in the last century," he sneered, "but your navy will be defenceless before a German fleet powered by the rays of twentieth-century science."

"Ah yes," Balfour replied, steepling his fingers as if prompted by a fresh recollection. "I am afraid to report that there has been an unfortunate fire at the Society for the Advancement of Science in Carlton House Terrace. The Metropolitan Fire Brigade was able to put out the conflagration before it reached the German Embassy, but in the basement of the Society, Professor Röntgen's laboratory was completely destroyed. The professor himself escaped with only minor injuries, but in the interests of his recovery I do not believe that he will be able to return to Germany for quite some time."

The Kaiser scowled, the hidden meaning behind Balfour's words instantly clear. There was no way that Great Britain would allow the secret of Röntgen's rays to leave her shores now. Professor Röntgen would be put under house arrest; the only experiments he would be allowed to conduct would be in the service of the British Empire.

"You will pay for your insolence," the Kaiser

hissed. "I swear I will bring this nation of shopkeepers and wayward children to heel. It may take a decade or more, but I promise you war."

"And Great Britain will be ready," King Edward growled in reply. "As long as I live, you will never set foot on these shores again. It goes without saying, Wilhelm, that you are no longer welcome at my coronation."

A malevolent cloud passed across the Kaiser's face, his right hand reaching for his empty scabbard. But before he could act, two Royal Marines stepped forward to seize hold of his arms.

"These men will accompany you to your quarters," Balfour declared as the Kaiser struggled in protest. "Once the King and the rest of the royal family have safely disembarked with the Crown Jewels, and our engineers have attended to the problem with the ship's engine, HMS *Revenge* will escort the *Hohenzollern* to the North Sea. I am sure you will be able to find your way home from there."

Still muttering darkly, the Kaiser was marched from the bridge, casting a murderous glance in Penelope's direction as she stood by Monty's side.

"We did it," the actor breathed.

His nephew now banished below decks, King Edward turned towards Monty and Penelope. He advanced towards them, his arms thrown wide in a gesture of thanks.

"Mr Flinch, I am forever in your debt. You have kept my family safe and through your endeavours rescued my throne. If it hadn't been for your timely sounding of the ship's horn in this maddening fog, then the *Hohenzollern* would have slipped unseen through the net cast by my rescue flotilla. I do not know how I can ever thank you." He stared at Monty with a look of wonder in his eyes. "Although I must admit I almost feel as though I am thanking myself."

Forgotten again, Penelope silently fumed.

"It was my honour, Your Majesty," Monty replied. He turned towards Penelope, presenting her to the King with a bow of his head. "And I couldn't have done any of it without the assistance of my niece, Miss Penelope Tredwell."

Behind his broad smile, a flicker of panic passed across the King's features. His gaze searched Penny's face for any sign of the strange glow he had seen when they last met in the dungeons of the Tower. Finally satisfied that she was restored to full health, he took her hand in his own in a heartfelt gesture of thanks.

"Miss Tredwell, you are a credit to the nation," he declared. "Is there any way I can show my appreciation?"

Penelope curtsied in reply, a shrewd smile slowly creeping across her lips.

"Well, there are a few things, Your Majesty..."

XXX

As the last chorus of "Zadok the Priest" faded away, an expectant silence fell over the Abbey. The gothic pews were filled with politicians and peers, foreign dignitaries and diplomats, representatives from all corners of the British Empire: its dominions, colonies, dependencies and protectorates. Most of Europe's royal families had been unable to return to London at such short notice to attend this hastily rearranged coronation, Kaiser Wilhelm the Second the most notable amongst these, but outside on the streets of Westminster the crowds waited, ready to acclaim their new King.

From her vantage point in a pew positioned halfway down the Abbey, Penelope saw the King take his seat on the Coronation Chair. Edward the Seventh was resplendent in robes of silver and gold, his balding head gleaming beneath the vaulted ceiling and stained-glass windows. Penny prodded Monty with her elbow, the actor lifting his head with a start.

"That could have been you, Monty," she whispered with a mischievous grin. Inclining his head towards hers, Monty met her suggestion with a sparkle in his eye.

"I am quite satisfied with the honour the King has already awarded me," he replied in a hushed whisper. "And that's *Sir* Montgomery Flinch to you, Miss Tredwell."

From over Monty's shoulder, Penny caught Alfie's gaze with a smile. Despite his new morning coat, the printer's assistant looked distinctly uncomfortable in these august surroundings. He returned Penny's smile with a blush, his ink-stained fingers itching to return to *The Penny Dreadful*'s offices to check the galley proofs of the September edition.

That had been the second way the King had shown his appreciation: lifting the royal decree banning the magazine's publication and in its place awarding them with a royal warrant of appointment. *The Penny Dreadful* was now the only magazine on the newsstands that could truthfully claim it was read by the King.

Seated on the Coronation Chair, Edward was presented with the Crown Jewels by the Archbishop of Canterbury. An orb, gleaming with precious stones and pearls, was placed with great ceremony in the King's right hand, the sound of the Archbishop's proclamation almost lost amongst the Abbey's pointed arches. Next came the royal ring, the sceptre and rod, before finally, with trembling hands, the Archbishop lifted the Imperial State Crown.

Edward leaned forward impatiently as the half-blind priest paused, peering blankly at a space just past the King's shoulder. "Get on with it," he hissed, impatient to begin his reign at last.

As if remembering where he was, the Archbishop slowly lowered the crown, little realising that it was the wrong way round as he placed it on Edward's head. But to the watching congregation this didn't matter one jot as a fanfare of trumpets sounded and a loud cry resounded from every corner of the Abbey.

"God save the King! God save the King!"

Penelope turned towards her guardian, Mr Wigram, who was wiping a tear from his eye as he joined in with these repeated shouts of acclamation. Next to him, the newest member of *The Penny Dreadful*'s staff was still bent over his sketchbook, the King's portrait slowly emerging as his pen moved confidently across the page. Feeling Penny's eyes upon him, Alexander Amsel glanced up, meeting her gaze with a shy smile.

Penny felt a familiar quickening of her heartbeat as she looked into Alexander's eyes. After taking his oath of allegiance to the King, Sea Cadet Amsel was now plain Alexander – *The Penny Dreadful*'s resident illustrator. As the final chorus of "God save the King" gradually faded away, the young artist gestured towards his sketchbook page.

"Perhaps we could include the King's portrait in the next edition of the magazine?" he suggested in a low voice. "I am sure the readers would want something to commemorate the coronation. But don't worry," he added, as if suddenly remembering himself. "I will first finish the cover illustration."

At this reminder, Penny's thoughts turned to the new story that was waiting for her on her desk back at *The Penny Dreadful*. With Montgomery Flinch's knighthood heralding his retirement from the world of fiction, it had been time for a new author to take the reins of the magazine. No more tales of the macabre; instead *The Penny Dreadful* was embracing the thrilling world of mystery with a new lead serial entitled *The Lady Investigates*.

This story told of a daring female detective, an amateur sleuth who was drawn into investigating a puzzling series of crimes. As she followed the clues across London, she uncovered a conspiracy that stretched from Paris to Berlin: a devilish plot to launch the world into war. With her quick wits and feminine intuition, the aristocratic investigator was soon on the trail of the mastermind behind this diabolical scheme, but could she convince the Ministers of His Majesty's

Government of the danger they faced before it was too late?

Under Alfie's jealous gaze, Alexander had presented Penelope with a mocked-up sketch of the cover to proclaim this new tale. With her dark hair swept high atop her head and the gleam of her pretty green eyes, the heroine of *The Lady Investigates* bore a striking resemblance to Penny herself. But it hadn't been this that had caused Penelope to feel a frisson of pride. Instead at the bottom of the page the cover line declared:

Introducing a dazzling new talent in the world of mystery fiction, *The Penny Dreadful* is proud to present *The Lady Investigates*, a thrilling tale from the pen of Miss Penelope Tredwell.

As the Abbey bells pealed out their glad tidings to the sound of cheers from the crowds outside, Penny lifted her face to the heavens with a smile. Montgomery Flinch had finally abdicated his literary throne. Long live Penelope Tredwell.

Acknowledgements

Many thanks to Mary Gillespie at the Tower of London, Jeremy Michell at the National Maritime Museum, Heather Johnson at the National Museum of the Royal Navy, Zoe English at the Marylebone Cricket Club and Lee Jackson for his wonderful website, *The Dictionary of Victorian London*, for their help with the research for this book. Thank you to my agent Lucy Juckes for her continued support, and a huge thanks to everyone at Nosy Crow, but especially Kirsty Stansfield, whose patience, encouragement and wise editorial counsel I found invaluable. With heartfelt thanks to my family for all their love and support, especially my children, Alex and Josie, and in loving memory of my nan, Olive.

Christopher Edge